# SCRIBINGS, VOL 3:
# METAMORPHOSIS

EDITED BY

JAMIE ALAN BELANGER

These are works of fiction. All names, characters, places, businesses, and incidents are purely fabrications from the author's imagination. Any re-semblance to actual persons (either living, dead, undead, or otherwise), places, companies, or even incidents is entirely coincidental.

"Third-Person Hero" ©2013 Jamie Alan Belanger
"Last Defender" ©2013 Shelli-Jo Pelletier
"Disruption" ©2013 D.L. Harvey
"Otherkin" ©2013 Steven Inman
"Four Degrees" ©2013 Timothy Lynch
"'Rose in Dreams" ©2013 Richard Veysey

Published in 2013 by Lost Luggage Studios, LLC
through Amazon CreateSpace.

ISBN: # 978-1-936489-16-9

Printed in the United States of America.

## ACKNOWLEDGEMENTS

Cover art designed by GPS using photography from Jamie Alan Belanger and D.L. Harvey

Interior glyph artwork by Shelli-Jo Pelletier

Cover art uses the following free fonts:
**Mekanik LET Plain** and **Vera Humana 95**

# Contents

# INTRODUCTION:
# Metamorphosis

C hange is the one constant in life. We grow, we age, we change. Throughout the courses of our lives, we are never the same from any one given moment to another. You constantly become older, and hopefully wiser. Every situation you enter, every person you meet, every book you read, every movie you watch... they all alter who you are, forever, for better or worse.

Sometimes the changes are subtle and gradual. They sneak up on you before you even realize what has happened. An old friend calls and over the course of the conversation realizes that you are not the person you used to be. It wasn't a sudden change; it was the culmination of all the little alterations you've undergone in the intervening years. You've experienced parts of life without that person and only he or she – now an outsider in your life – can see what it has done to you. This type of change is natural, something you in-corporate into your life without even realizing what is happening.

Not all change is subtle, however. Some changes are sudden and so pro-found they shake us to the very core of who we are. These changes come from situations like the accidents we see on the road every day, the criminals turning the unaware into victims, the deaths of those we hold dear, and the chance encounters that bring new people into our lives. It need not be an event that happens to you; just knowing the person affected can be enough to trigger a change.

Rarely does it matter if the change is physical, mental, or emotional, as all three aspects of our selves are intertwined. After one terrible or glorious moment, you are suddenly more cautious, less trusting, more aware, less car-ing. In some way, you've changed. Sometimes the change is small. Some-times you are completely transformed, and like an insect or amphibian, you undergo an irreversible metamorphosis. You are no longer the person you used to be.

However it comes, change is always inevitable. You can't prevent it. You can't avoid it.

How we deal with change shapes who we become.

# THIRD-PERSON HERO

## BY JAMIE ALAN BELANGER

**B**ronson Alistar. It's hard to find anyone these days who hasn't heard the name, or who doesn't know the allegations and derision associated with it. For a time, he was everyone's hero. He did to the American sport of baseball what few dreamed possible: he renewed interest in it. He showed that humans were still capable of greatness. When he stepped up to bat, he didn't bother to point. He didn't need to demonstrate his arrogance. He knew he'd hit it out of the park. The pitcher knew as well. Most pitchers stopped trying to slip balls past him. Some rookies would still try, and there were running bets for years about who could actually succeed. The catchers, well, they stopped trying as well. Most took a break, sitting to the side to watch the greatest player alive do his thing. The ball would slice through the air, and Bronson Alistar would swing. Perfect motion. Perfect tempo. Flawless precision. The crowd would go silent, holding their breaths until they heard the telltale crack of his bat, then they'd cheer as the ball shot into the sky. In most cities, fans in the parking lot would try to catch the ball. Even the Duplex Dome in Tokyo, with its double-sized diamond, was no match for Bronson Alistar.

He was a hero. Well, until people found out *how* he was playing so well.

The allegations started as a routine doping investigation in 2059. They found no evidence of drugs. They found an augmentation. The International Baseball League had outlawed muscle augmentations years prior, hoping to avoid players with unfair advantages. They continuously scanned players for such augments. But it wasn't until Bronson Alistar was scanned head-to-toe that they found where his augmentation was – in his head. He hit the ball flawlessly every time because his eyes saw it coming, the computer installed in his head calculated the trajectory, computed the physics, and then directed the muscles in his arms to swing the bat at just the right speed, in just the right location, so it would hit the ball at just the right angle and velocity. Every pitch. Every swing. Every time.

Considering what this revelation did to the sport of baseball, you'd probably call me crazy for trying to do a similar thing to the sport of competitive gymnastics. And maybe I am. But I've earned this chance to shine. After seeing what Bronson Alistar had gone through, I believe I can get away with it. He was too perfect, too flawless. All you have to do is fail, once in a while. Not in a big face-planted-into-concrete sort of way. Something small would do, like, say, perhaps you reach for one of the uneven bars and just happen to miss. Or a little falter when planting your feet on the mat after doing a balance bar routine.

It's those little things that make you appear... well... *human*.

Looking at myself in the mirror, I can see a gymnast's body. Perfect form, not too tall, nice muscle tone. I'm wearing my least favorite leotard, an ugly neon green piece that I've learned to live with. I tried to rip it (even tried cutting it with scissors once) and burn it (the neighbor's welding torch didn't even scorch it) but the damn thing is invincible. My mother says it's "age ap-propriate," like wrapping a sixteen-year-old in neon green was the most natu-ral thing in the world. I complained to Father, and he purchased several other leotards for me, ones that I like much more. But I can't throw this one away. The simple fact is that Mother loves when I wear it. My coach says my moth-er wore it often, back when she was competing. I've seen the videos, several times, too many times. I would never wear this thing to a competition. I don't even like wearing it at practice, but doing so makes her smile, so I make that one small concession.

I turn to look at my profile. My breasts are small, just barely there, and almost invisible behind the glare of this fabric. If I take after my mother, I don't suspect I'll have much to worry about there. Not for the duration of a gymnast's career, at least. I pivot and look at my backside. Again, perfect. Flawless tone. I strike a pose and my ponytail bounces. Smiling, I inspect my facial features. Two white rows of teeth, high cheekbones, light eyeshadow accentuates my natural iris color. I was born to be a gymnast. I'm sure of it. I am my mother's daughter. It's too bad I inherited my father's awkward clum-siness. There, on the back of my thigh, a fresh bruise from practice, bright and purple. Just a few days old. I exhale and shake my head. I won't give up. All I want is to be the gymnast I know I was born to be.

In the background of my room, the video hits the end and starts again. It's me on the screen, at practice a few days ago, tumbling and twisting above a balance beam. Then a loud *thwack* as my leg hits the beam. Clumsiness. Just like my father, I find furniture in the dark with my shins. I slam my fin-gers in car doors. I always tie my hair back in ponytails or braids, not be-cause I like the look, but because I know if I don't then my hair will get caught in something. I'm far too awkward to do what I love, and it's tearing me apart. My body shakes with a fresh wave of rage as I watch myself on the video. I'm trying to rise from the mat, but my arms slip and I slam back down, planting my face firmly. If that had been concrete, I'd probably have a broken nose, or an eye to match my purple thigh. My mother's voice is cap-tured in the video at this moment, barely audible but obviously disappointed. The camera is set down and I see my mother rush to console me. As the tears course down my face, I rub my thigh and peer at the camera.

"There," I say, pointing at the screen. "*That's* the exact moment I had the idea."

In the corner of the screen, the sad face of my friend Alice nods. I've known her for years, longer than anyone else besides my parents. She's always been there for me. My best friend, my confidant. She knows everything about me. This plan is just one more secret for us to share.

On the video, not even a second after the idea hit me, my tears stop as if I turned off the faucet. My head cocks to the side and a sly smile worms its way into my countenance.

"I believe your idea is possible, Jill," Alice says, "with the right operation and software."

"And I know I can get away with it," I reply, staring at myself on the video.

Alice nods. "I believe so too. You will be amazing."

I thank her and post my latest video to my social feed. Edited, of course. I'm not going to let my online presence be a testament to my failures. Alice posts a positive comment soon after the video appears, then she logs off. I close the app and return my attention to the mirror.

Though I hadn't told her, I've scheduled the surgery for tomorrow. My own little augment. My own perfect secret. It actually took me longer to think of a reasonable cover than it did to decide on getting the augment. Slipping the cover past my father was easy. He's been working on a big case for weeks, and spending many hours at the firm where he works. He was so eager to end the conversation that he agreed before I could even finish my explanation. My regular doctor knows my father is a lawyer. I mentioned a few key phrases I'd researched online and she acquiesced almost as fast as Father did. I've heard Father complain about privacy laws before, but I certainly have no complaints about them. Mother, well, she can barely work the camera I asked her to bring to practice (and believe me, that's quite a source of embarrassment these days!). This augment was way above her head. My father had already agreed, and so she assumed he understood and felt it was a decent enough idea.

I just hope nobody learns the truth. I want to be a hero, not another Bronson Alistar. I look at my reflection in the mirror, brush the light brown bangs from my face, and blow a kiss. Then I raise my hands and spin on my toes, extend my leg, and smack it into my desk.

*   *   *

"Jilly?" A voice, somewhere, everywhere. Masculine, familiar. "Jill honey, are you all right? I think she's coming out of it..."

I open my eyes to see a blurry version of my father leaning over me. "Dad?" I squeak. I'm actually surprised he's here, given all the time he's been spending at work lately.

"I'm here, sweetheart," he says. "How are you feeling?"

Room spinning. Vision a little blurred. I groan in response.

He frowns. "Is this normal?"

"Quite normal," my doctor says. "Any visual augmentation will require a few days to adjust."

"It's just that... I was so worried when she told me about her fall in practice the other day," my father says. "If her contacts had been dislodged when she hit the mat, or—"

I can hear my mother, in the background, a sharp intake of breath. She is probably reliving that incident.

"Of course," my doctor replies. "She will never need to wear glasses or contacts again. She'll be fine in an hour or two. For now, she could use some rest." She ushers my father out of my view. I can hear her talking to my parents outside the room.

I blink a few times and prop myself on my elbows. I focus my gaze on the bathroom door for several seconds, until the blurriness fades. Then I turn to look at a chair off to my left, which bears a short stack of clothes I recognize to be mine. I look up, at the telescreen, which is tuned to some cartoon I hadn't seen before. My vision is already clearing. Next I look at the small window and the tree outside. My vision darkens as I focus on the tree. The doctor returns and sits on the bed. She places a finger on my chin, turns my head toward her and shines a light in my eyes. My vision adjusts quickly and filters the incoming light. "Perfect!" she says. "Well, now you no longer need sunglasses either."

"And..." I say.

"Yes, that too," she responds. "You teenagers and your technology. Carrying a phone just wasn't enough, was it? I guess it will be easier to keep in touch with your friends with a wireless T-Jack in your head. Can't say I would want that for myself, though."

I close my eyes and pretend to be tired. Dull lines come into view, asking me to type my login credentials for the hospital's Internet connection. After several seconds, the lines fade into darkness. "I just..." I start, then clear my throat and sigh. "Just want to keep in touch with friends when I'm supposed to be practicing, that's all. I don't want anyone to know about that. Might be some problems in school with it." I'd just thought about that one. They took cheating pretty seriously. What if they decided to kick me out?

She snorts and sighs, almost at the same time. "Don't worry, I've sealed your records according to the Privacy Act of 2068. Not even your parents can get into them. As for school, well, there's an option on your menu to turn off the data connection. It's the last entry on the list. Get in the habit of doing that before school and you should never have a problem. Nobody will ever know."

*Except you*, I think. I'm hoping she's serious about sealing the records. But I can't help but think this is my first mistake...

*   *   *

"Thank-you-for-your-pur-chase," the automated vendor says in perfect yet halting English. I start to respond with some pleasantry but stop myself – she is, after all, just a glorified chat script. Give her any input not in her list and she'll just present a menu of options. It's amazing how rudimentary these store assistants still are. You can get more sophisticated conversations out of a child's toy.

I accelerate into the flow of traffic and move into a virtual alleyway. I'm

still not used to the hues and motion blur, but I've been told that will get better in time. It's only been three weeks since I've had this wireless T-Jack installed. Can't expect to use it efficiently right out of the gate. I've spent my
whole life connecting to the Net using older, slower, less efficient ways – a
remote pointed at a telescreen, or typing on a keyboard at my desk, or wearing itchy data gloves and bulky goggles. With this new connection, I just
have to stand near a wireless access point. Those are nearly everywhere.
Close my eyes, log in, and I'm connected to the rest of the world. Much
faster, much easier. I'm sure I'll get used to it, soon, and will probably never
use my computer or telescreen again.

A little ways into the alley, I stop. In my virtual hands, I'm holding my
purchase: a small program for home monitoring. A flick of the wrist installs
the software. It appears to work, or at least as well as any software that
doesn't crash the moment you try to use it. I don't have a camera to attach to,
so I can't know for sure. There's a short list of cameras that it functions with,
all sold (at considerable prices) by the same vendor I had just visited. I still
had money in my personal bank account, and could afford a few of their
cameras, but my plan required a different approach.

There's a darker corner of the Net, not too far from here.

I move away from the traffic and push into the air, soaring above the city
grid. I scan the digital horizon. All the major corporations have a presence
here, like they do at every public node. A few local businesses have buildings
here as well, but the corporations made sure their buildings were much smaller and segregated into a special district so most people wouldn't be able to
find them. Near the perimeter of the virtual city, I see my target. Twelve
buildings that look unimposing, nondescript. From the ground, it's just another little district that most people would cruise past and never pay attention to.
From the air, the buildings are arranged in a pattern, showing a symbol that
the hackers adopted long ago as a symbol of defiance. Even the authorities
don't go here unless they have a specific purpose.

Landing nearby is easy, but this is a dangerous place to be, especially
with hardware installed inside my head. Any half-decent hacker could infil-
trate my head and turn me into a vegetable in three seconds flat.

"Hello," Alice says, her unexpected presence makes me jump. "Did you get the software?"

"Alice? What are you doing here?"

"I was looking for you," she replies. "You were not in the usual places and I know it is too late for you to be at the gym. Where are you going now? Can I come?"

"Somewhere dangerous," I say. "I need to get a crack for this software."

She looks around with a neutral expression. "Here?"

"You remember Bill Jacobs?"

"From school? You had a crush on him in third grade."

"Shut up!" I say, feeling my real-life cheeks flush.

Alice smiles in response. "Sorry."

"Bill Jacobs hangs out around here. He knows about all this software cracking and hacker stuff."

"So you will ask him for help?"

"I'm going to *pay* him for help."

Alice nods. "That should work, but what about school? You do not normally spend time with him. Not since third grade, at least."

I hadn't thought of that. Before I can respond, Alice waves her hand. Her avatar shimmers for a moment, then turns into a copy of someone I can see off in the distance. "How did you do that?" I ask.

"It is easy, here. I will change you now, and Bill will not recognize you."

"Okay," I say, getting a little excited.

Alice reaches out and touches me. I can feel a tingle of warmth snake through my body. She pulls her hand back and smiles. "Done," she says. She waves her arm and a mirror appears beside us, showing a reflection of two unfamiliar people.

"How did you learn to do that?" I ask.

"I read a lot."

"This reminds me of all the times we played dress-up games."

"Yes," Alice says. "That was a long time ago. Shall we go to Bill now?"

We move a short ways down the virtual street toward a squat, faux brick building. Some trick of the graphics texture makes the bricks appear to be sliding around as you shift your vision. Inside are two avatars, chatting in an encrypted stream. The sound reminds me of a science fiction cartoon I saw in the hospital, an odd screeching noise that varies in pitch every so often. One of them turns to me when I enter. He waves his arm and I can feel the place close around me. The light dims and his friend grows silent. Neither of these looks anything like Bill. Actually, the one who waved his arm looks a little like a Japanese cartoon demon.

"What do you two want?" he asks.

"Are you—" I start to ask, then stop a moment, trying to remember what his online hacker alias was. "I mean, I'm looking for 'The Overlord.' " Boys and their egos.

"Maybe," the friend replies. "What are you looking for?"

"I just bought Surveillance Pro 4.5 and was looking for a way to—"

"Wait," he says. He moves closer and waves his arms. I feel a tingle, then I'm pulled closer to him. My heart beats faster. Alice, thankfully, is quiet. Last thing I need now is another reference to the third grade. He reaches a hand inside of my avatar. Feels weird, like a tingling in my stomach indicating I ate something bad. He removes his hand, says something in gibberish, frowns, then waves his arms again. "There. Do you understand me now?"

"Yes."

"I've encrypted our connection, and scanned you. *Now* we can deal. So, go on."

"I-I've been looking for a way to control other cameras with Surveillance Pro."

"I see," he says. I get the impression that he's pausing to size me up, but his avatar never shifts position. "Yeah, their cameras are still way overpriced. But the crack ain't cheap either. If you're only looking to control three or four cameras, buy theirs."

"My needs are for a few more than that."

"Euros or Yen?"

"Euros."

A number flashes in the lower portion of my vision. Crime pays better than any high school job he ever could have gotten in the real world.

"Includes installation," he says.

"All right. How do I pay it?"

"Wire it to this account," he says, reaching out toward me. While holding onto my virtual arm, he flashes a number on the screen. A window opens, asking for verification. All the fields are filled out, including the amount. I read the number again and wince. It's a lot of money, but I have enough. I think. I press the button to confirm. The transfer doesn't take more than a few seconds. "Thanks," he says, then, still holding onto me, he leans forward. "This is going to feel strange."

It does. Like fire, crawling up my arms. My avatar doesn't flinch. My real body shudders so much I can hear my bed's headboard scrape against the wall.

"Relax," he says, "I'm a straight-shooter. There are some shady people around here, but I ain't one of 'em. Don't worry, I've been doing this kind of thing for years." The fire subsides, replaced by an eerie tingle. "Good, better. This won't take long." He twists my arm a little, and I feel another tingling surge pulse through my body. He releases me and moves back. "Done. Enjoy."

"Thanks," I say.

Then I'm propelled out of his building and left standing in the virtual street, surrounded by socializing avatars. Alice is standing beside me, back to using her normal avatar, with that usual bored expression on her face. I ignore her and reach for the disconnection command.

*   *   *

My room comes into focus a little quicker this time. On the telescreen, the video of my last practice, still as clumsy as ever. *The next one will be better.* I turn on my camera and place it on the dresser, aiming it at my bed. I sit on the bed and cross my legs, taking a deep breath. The camera stares at me, a single red light blinking to announce that it is on. In the mirror I can see a reflection of the viewscreen, a hazy version of me staring straight ahead. I close my eyes and the Net login prompt appears. Brushing it away, I open a list of programs, choosing Surveillance Pro. It starts, announcing that it is now the "Overlord Edition" of the program. Better work. I've spent a few thousand Euros on this modification. Thankfully, it was *my* money, and my parents don't closely monitor my personal account. They pay my allowance into it automatically, and between practice and school I don't have any time to go shopping. Still, I should have been saving for college...

I shake my head and take a deep breath. It *will* work. And then if – *when* – it does, I'll replenish that account with my first endorsement deal. Replenish and then some.

The program loads and I let it scan for local cameras. It finds mine and I select it. And there I am – sitting on my bed, seen through the camera's lens. I open my eyes and see that my left eye is showing the camera's view, while the right one sees my room from my perspective. I move my arms, focusing my attention on the left eye's view. Disorienting, at first, but the more I move the more fluid my motions become. I giggle and it sounds odd, warped, with a hint of an echo. A quick check of the program's options yields a simple check box, which I select, to disable the audio feed. I move my head, looking away from the mirror. The colors are over-saturated. My pink wallpaper looks almost red through the camera's eye. I find another option to adjust the color temperature, and spend far too long examining my room in the grayscale, sepia, warm, and vivid modes. I find the room looks best in the "cool" mode. Rather funny, considering that's one of my father's favorite slang words for things he likes. Closing my right eye makes the effect a little more usable. I brush my hair, and seeing a stray piece of lint on my back, I reach back and grab it.

I spend most of the day doing this, moving around my room, watching myself through the unfailing eye of the camera. When my mother calls me for dinner, I sever the connection and take a deep breath. The world seems to sway a little. Another deep breath and things smooth out. I head downstairs, a little more exuberance in my step.

*       *       *

At practice the next day, I insist that my mother bring my camera. She's used to this by now. I've been having her record my practices for weeks. *I need to see where I'm failing, so I can fix it.* That's been the same line I say, every day. She agrees with her sad little smile. She wants me to be the best gymnast I can be. I think she wants to live a second gymnast's career through me vicariously, as if she could recapture her rapidly fading youth. At least that's the impression I get the few times I succeed and she makes me watch her old competition videos... with that ugly neon green leotard, at every competition, and her glowing smile. She talks about Regionals, and Nationals, and her failed bid for the Olympic team. And every time she pulls out the camera at practice, her face takes on that "Oh, honey, I'll love you no matter what" look that I'm growing to despise, because somewhere underneath that expression is another that is watching and waiting and hoping for me to shine.

Today will be different. With *this* practice, my life will change.

"Start with uneven bars," my coach says in his thick Eastern European accent. He's adopted the same expression as my mother. Damn near bored. Might as well just admit to my face that he's only here because my parents keep paying him. He's got other students who are doing well in the local competitions. I'm sure he'd rather work with stars all day long, but instead he gets me, seven days a week for the past few years. It must be painful to watch such a clumsy gymnast. He points at the uneven bars, as if I wasn't paying attention. "That's where you need most work," he says.

He's not kidding. Every practice for the past two weeks, I've started with the uneven bars. And on some of those days, I've ended on the uneven bars, and gone home with fresh bruises that stung something fierce. One day I hit the lower bar with my abdomen, spun around it, and went headfirst into the mat. Knocked me out instantly. My mom fainted, convinced I had been killed. My coach had to nurse us both back to consciousness. And when I came to, my entire vision was filled with his face. Concern? Hardly. Disappointment? You bet. And that disappointment was mirrored in my mother's face when he had moved away.

Standing before the equipment, I close my eyes and take a deep breath, slowly stretching while I connect to the camera. I feel for the chalk, patting my hands and trying not to inhale the cloud I'm making. I open my left eye and can see myself. I drop the chalk ball and jump, grabbing the upper bar, and start my routine. Twisting, turning, I get to the first troublesome spot. This is where I fell, just two days ago. Nearly cracked a rib. I close my right eye and concentrate on the big picture. I release the bar and twist my body backward, just the way I had – hey! I see my problem immediately. I'm not overextending and missing the lower bar. I'm *under-extending.* I stretch my arms and my body shifts in mid-air. I feel the bar hit my hands and grab tight.

"Good, good," my coach says, sounding a little less bored.

My legs tuck in close to my body, gathering momentum on the next swing. I release the bar and spin to the side, rolling in the air, and reach out. I can see the problem, clear as day. Now I *am* overextending. I move my arms in toward my body and grab the upper bar.

"Very good," my coach says, watching with renewed interest. "Now for finish..."

I raise my legs and flip over, still holding the bar, then tuck them in again. I waver a little. The motion is a little too fast to see it clearly with this external view. I do an extra twist on the bar to regain the lost momentum. When I can see I've reached the apex of my height, I release the bar and pitch forward. My body twists once, twice, three times, and then I stick my feet out, straight down, planting them onto the mat. I arch my back and strike the winner's pose.

"Good dismount," my coach says. He clears his throat and gestures to the next obstacle. "Now, balance beam..."

*   *   *

Practice continues much like this for the next few weeks. The external view does amazing things for my form. After the first week, I add a second camera, propped on the floor and aimed in my general direction. With some difficulty, I manage to link my mom's camera to one eye and mine to the other. To say it's disorienting is quite an understatement. At first, at least. I fall once, slamming my shin into the balance beam. I take a deep breath and guide my body back on. I can see my coach turn to hide his expression, but he looks right at my camera in the process. He's worried, a little upset. At least that's an improvement over boredom.

I take a deep breath and focus on the task at hand. I jump, twisting to the side. I can see my eyes looking toward my camera, glazed and lifeless. I try to tell myself it's just a look of extreme concentration. Reviewing the tapes later, I can see that's not true. They look dead. It's a normal look, actually. You can see it on dozens of faces in any cafe in any city. It's the look of the logged-in, the people who are physically sipping overpriced lattes while mentally connected to the Internet. The eyes look dead because they aren't being used by the body. I start to squint during my routines, which makes the problem less noticeable. Judges look for out-of-place things like that; any reason to deduct points.

Using two cameras helps me find another flaw in my routines. I was getting used to performing for my mom's camera, which made some of my poses and twists look two-dimensional. Using a second perspective, I'm able to get the hang of doing three poses when I finish a routine. Stretch and pose front, left, then right. My coach is pleased. My mother is ecstatic. Another fall in the same practice results in that same familiar look of disappointment from my coach, accompanied by a colorful comment from my mother, under her breath, apparently oblivious to the fact that she's holding a camera. I'm glad I decided to turn off the audio feed in Surveillance Pro. I don't need to hear words like that when I'm trying to practice. I decide not to watch the footage anymore.

\* \* \*

Two days later, while practicing on the balance beam, the vision in my left eye blinks out mid-jump. The external view of me is replaced by a rather large, grinning image of Alice. "What are you doing logged in at this time of day?" she asks. The audio completes the disorientation and I fall, hitting the beam on the way down. I yelp and grab my thigh where it hit the beam. "That did not sound good," Alice says.

"Alice?" I whisper. "How did you–"

"Am I interrupting something?" she asks. "You should be in practice."

"I *am*," I grit my teeth and rub my aching thigh. My coach slaps a small pad on the area and presses hard. The pad hums and the pain subsides. I close my eyes so he can't see the dead look. *How did you override my camera view?* I think. The words appear below her image as I think them.

"You were logged into the Internet," Alice responds. "I started a video chat connection and it was accepted. I am sorry. You have not been online in weeks. We usually talk every day. I missed you."

"That feels better, yes?" my coach asks.

"Much better," I respond.

"Pardon?" Alice asks.

*Talking to coach,* I think, watching the words appear. *I have to practice.*

Alice looks sad. She disconnects without saying goodbye. I terminate the Internet connection and break the connections to the cameras.

Opening my eyes, I see my coach, looking concerned. He removes the pad and stands. "Continue," he says.

I stand and get back on the beam.

*     *     *

The next week, I manage to perform my entire routine, start to finish, without a single error. I still haven't quite figured out how to hide my lifeless eyes, but squinting certainly appears to help. I make the last turn on the balance beam routine, bounce once and flip into the air, twist, and plant my feet on the mat. I strike a pose for my coach, my mother, and the camera propped in the corner.

"Very good, Jillian," my coach says. "You are ready."

I can't think of a clever response that doesn't sound arrogant, so I merely smile as I bow my head and close the connection to the cameras. I feel a small wave of vertigo hit when the connection is severed. I'm getting used to that problem, but I don't expect it will ever go away completely.

"Do you *feel* ready?" he asks.

I raise my eyes to meet his, letting him see the anticipation. "I am ready," I say.

"Good," he says, smiling. "Regionals are next week, and I'm proud to say I feel you are ready. I have already entered you in competition, at request of your mother. Is necessary to do well at regional competition. I think you know what happens after that..."

"Olympics," I respond. A shiver of excitement tingles its way up my spine. My chance to shine before the whole world. Win a medal, gain respect, be a hero. Everything I ever wanted. Everything my mom ever wanted – for me, for her. My chance to be what she failed to be. I glance at my camera, sitting there, lifeless lens staring back at me. With all the high-tech cameras pointed at me, there was no chance for failure at any competition. *I'm going to be a star.*

"No, not yet," my coach says. I had forgotten he was there. He wraps a meaty arm around my shoulder and squeezes. "Eventually, perhaps. Regionals, *then* Nationals competitions. Olympics come much later. But I suppose time will go by quickly. You could be star of 2072 Summer Olympics. Your country's greatest little athlete. A prime example of what people can still achieve with proper training and hard work. But first, you must concentrate on *Regionals*. You are sixteen. Time is precious. This is last opportunity. Keep focus on what comes *next*, not on what could be, some day, maybe, in future. Da? Good."

He gives me another squeeze, then releases his grip and goes to talk with my mother. I collect my camera and, admiring my reflection in the lens, I walk into the locker room door.

*   *   *

One day before the Regionals competition, I walk into the hall with my coach and my mother on either side of me. The lights overhead, which should be glaring down on us, are off today. It's a beautiful day outside, and the windows above let the natural light filter in. This lets me see the entire auditorium, from floor mats to steel beams. Gymnasts from nearby counties cover the floor mats, stretching, warming up, practicing. I'm wearing that ugly green leotard, in the hopes that the glare distracts my competition and appeases my mother at the same time. Plus, if I wear it *today*, there's no way she could insist on me wearing it *tomorrow*.

Glancing around the hall, I pick my targets. One camera, behind where the judges will sit, looking over their table at the balance beam. It gives a perfect side view of the beam, while also ensuring that I know exactly what the judges are seeing. The other camera is in a far corner, giving a good angle that will help with the routine's second half. There are other cameramen still moving their equipment, talking to workers in the media booth about their placement. I take a moment to connect to each camera. There are no issues with the connections, and nobody seems to have noticed my intrusions. While stretching my legs on the mat near my coach, I make all the choices for angles that I will need tomorrow.

A man walks onto the judge's platform and asks for everyone's attention. He explains the rules of today's elimination rounds. There are too many gymnasts entered for tomorrow's competition, so today he will personally score each performance and select fewer than half of us to come back tomorrow. My coach looks a little worried. My mother is sweating. I'm calm and confident.

The first round of eliminations goes slowly. The judge chooses the uneven bars as the first event. Four girls lose their grips and he sends them home. The rest get little more than a nod and a few quick taps on his tablet. I connect to two of the cameras and perform my routine flawlessly. When I dismount, I can see my coach in the background giving my mother one of those awkward side-hugs.

The second round is the balance beam. I have to pick an alternate camera since the judge is standing by the table and blocking my view. My performance here is perfect as well. Some of the other girls are starting to look worried. Another twelve girls are sent home after this event. The last girl to get on the beam slips and falls to the mat. She gets sent home without even getting a chance to start her routine.

When the judge starts the third round, the vault, I have to try several cameras as the remaining gymnasts are blocking some of the view. This won't be a problem tomorrow, as all the competitors would be on the sidelines, or in the locker rooms. Today is just a mass of young girls standing on the mats. The judge has to call my name twice before I realize it's my turn. I get in position, select the two best cameras I can find, and run. At the end of the runway, I jump, hit the springboard, push off the vaulting table, and launch into the air. Once I'm above the other girls, I can see myself clearly in the camera's view. The cameraman manning one of the cameras turns slightly to follow me as I twist in the air. Someone should give *him* a medal. As I approach the mat, I extend my legs and plant them, then pose.

As the judge starts calling names for performing in the final round – the floor exercise – I count the girls remaining. I count them again and get the same number. The judge has already eliminated enough girls, yet the preliminaries go on. My coach and my mother don't seem to have noticed. Everyone appears to have been caught up in the spirit of the competition.

My name is called. I approach the mat and the music I've selected (or, rather, that my mother had selected) starts. A quick turn, a few dance moves, and I'm off. In the middle of my first jump, the vision in my left eye turns black. In its place is a short list of notifications. Alice apparently has posted a comment about me competing and some of the kids from school responded. I forgot to disable the network connection again! I stumble, twisting as I fall, but manage to catch myself. I blink hard and the camera's vision comes back, but I'm linked to a different camera now. Can't help that, I just picked the first one on the list. I didn't have time to be picky.

I continue my routine, heart beating a little faster than it should. I move around the mat, smiling and flashing my blank, glassy eyes at the other girls, who are close enough to notice but too self-involved to care. The song nears its end and while turning into my last spin, my other eye cuts out. In the background, with my good eye, I can see the guy replacing the camera's battery. I miss my mark and fall to the mat. Before anyone realizes what is happening, I shut that eye and rotate my shoulder, plopping into a sitting

position. The song ends and I strike a casual pose. My coach frowns, knowing that ending was not a part of the routine. My mother scolds me later,
wondering out loud why I would risk elimination for something so silly. She
makes me promise that I won't try anything like that at the actual competition.

Later that night, I connect to the Net, and check my messages. I have
fourteen, all from Alice. She's worried that I haven't posted any videos lately.
She's posted a few comments on my social feed, and bumped some old
videos. She sent two apologies for interrupting my practice the other day. I
send her a pleasant response with some smiley faces and disconnect.

*　　*　　*

The crowd is enormous, much larger than anything I ever imagined.
Even just with light conversations they manage to fill the entire building with
a wall of sound. My heart is beating faster than usual. I smooth the fabric on
my leotard – one that *I've* chosen, *my* favorite – as I sit on the sidelines,
watching other young girls competing. The judges watch in silence, then bow
their heads to jot notes on little tablets. The next girl is announced, and she
approaches the balance beam. She launches onto it, lurches, and almost falls.
The crowd holds their breaths. In that moment of silence, she recovers with
little more than a small falter. But I saw it. I'm sure the judges have as well.

My mother checks my hair for the tenth time, tightening the clasps that
hold it in place. Her hands are shaking, and she almost manages to undo the
bun containing my hair. My coach is saying something encouraging, but I'm
trying my best to ignore him. My chance to shine is next. I know what I need
to do. I scan the crowd and try to comprehend what the announcers had said
earlier: thirty thousand people. The number is boggling. I've never seen this
many people in one place before. Someone once said that some goals are so
worthy that even to fail would be glorious. I get a sense of that, here. Falling
and hurting myself in front of my coach and my parents is one thing. But
here? Or at the Olympics? Just getting invited to these competitions is an
honor. But to fail–

I take a deep breath and hold it. *No*, I think. *I won't fail. Not here. I can't.*

The girl on the beam finishes, jumping and doing a single twist before planting her feet on the mat. The crowd cheers and awaits the judging. I stand and take a deep breath. My name is called. While approaching the beam, the previous girl's scores are announced. She did well, but that falter had cost her a medal. She'd most likely be crying herself to sleep tonight.

I stop before the beam and close my eyes. I double-check that my network connection has been disabled and pick my cameras. When I open my eyes, I've tapped into the two cameras I had chosen. One of the judges tells me I may begin, and I do, jumping forward and planting both hands on the edge of the beam. I slowly bring my legs up and over. Perfect form, flawless precision. I see a judge in the lower part of the view as he makes a note. I can't quite read his screen, not that I need that distraction. I arch my back and touch my feet to the beam, then push off with my hands and bring my torso upright. I immediately pitch forward and do a somersault. I almost miss my foot placement, but the wide view from the corner camera helps me land it well.

The rest of the routine goes quickly. The crowd doesn't breathe for most of it. Even some of the judges look spellbound as they watch my body contort over the beam. Every move precise, every hand and foot placement exact. When I dismount, my double twist earns the thunderous approval of the crowd. I break the connections to the cameras, open my eyes wide, and pose for the judges, for the crowd, for my corner camera. I return to my coach to await my score.

But I already know the score. I had watched my own performance. There was no error, no falter, no problems evident. The only thing that still concerned me was whether or not the judges had seen the lifeless look in my eyes. Even that wasn't much of a concern. There was so much lighting in this place that even *I* could see reflections sparkling in my eyes.

The scores are read to another round of thunderous crowd approval. One of the judges had made a small deduction. The rest had seen perfection and had rewarded it. The probability of any of these other girls beating that score was small. If I could perform the other events this well, I'd have the highest scores ever seen in the history of this competition. At least, that's what my coach is saying. I smile at him and accept another of his shoulder-embraces. He smells a little like vodka. I guess that's just his way of calming nerves before watching a competition.

"Next will be vault," my coach says. "Then uneven bars, then floor exercise. You remember routine?" He sounds concerned. "Routine with *correct* ending?"

"I remember."

My name is called first for the vault. I approach the runway and close my eyes, breathing deeply and syncing my view with the cameras. I don't like the angle I get from the corner camera, so I link to another. Slightly better. At least I'll have a good view of the landing from there. Not so much for the approach. I open my eyes and take off, running as fast as I can, then leap and land on the springboard. Leaning forward, I plant my hands on the vaulting table, compress my arms, and push with all my might. I can see the form in my left eye – perfect height, more than I've ever achieved in practice. I twist, spinning to the side, then pitch my body into a somersault. At the last possible moment, I extend my legs and land on the mat. I was right. The new camera gave a perfect angle for the landing. I raise my arms to pose for the crowd. This time I do four poses. The crowd's cheers are starting to stab at my ears, the pitch is almost too much. I love it, but wonder if I should consider an aural augment to defend against this sort of thing.

When I get back to my mother, she hugs me, more pleased than I've ever seen her. Like she thought my balance beam performance was some sort of fluke. No, not a fluke. This is the *new* me. Confident. Talented. Heroic. I don't even bother listening for my score. My mother's reaction tells me enough. The rest of the girls take their turns as I scan the crowd. Something about this whole situation just feels right. I'd been working for this chance to shine for so many years. I'm so glad that I finally got the chance to live it.

The rest of the competition flies by, almost literally if you saw my floor exercise. Felt like my feet barely touched the floor at all, I moved and twisted with such alacrity and grace. Even that one stubborn note-taking judge finally caved and awarded a perfect score. When the rest of the girls had all finished their routines, the judges talked for several minutes and announced the winners.

I approach the platform with mild trepidation to accept my medal. Gold. First place. Two days ago, none of these people had any idea who I was. Now I was standing on the highest platform, waving to the cheering people in the crowd. I take the time to wave and smile at each camera, partly to thank them for their contribution to my performance. I know at least one of them will transmit that recording of me off to be processed so it can appear on every local kid's cereal box for the next few weeks. I picture myself on the front of those boxes, waving at random children as they eat their breakfasts and dream of doing exceptional deeds. When I finish posing for each camera, I return my attention to the crowd. Even the people holding banners proclaiming their love and support for other competitors are clapping. *For me.* I exchange hugs with the girls who won second and third place, then hit the showers.

When I exit the shower, I enable my network connection and see a text message, from Alice, congratulating me on the win. She's already posted about it on my social feed, so all the kids at school know too. The video she linked to has already received two hundred comments. While thinking of something nice to say in response, my thoughts appear in the comment box. *Thanks so much everyone.* Nothing special. Generic, yet gracious enough. I post the comment.

I emerge from the locker room to see my mother and coach talking with someone new.

"Jill," my mother says, "this is Mister Hanson. He, well- he has something he wants to ask you."

My skin tingles. *A fan? Or does he suspect...* Before I can even finish contemplating the implications, he extends his hand. I grasp it.

"Your performance today was excellent. Amazing. Absolutely incredible," he says.

"Thank you," I say. My heart threatens to punch through my chest.

"I was wondering if you would consider providing a demonstration at tomorrow's Anderton Invitational? I'm sorry, I know this is very short notice.

It's a small event, mostly something for soliciting charity donations from lo-cal businesses. But I do know some people there would be very interested in seeing you perform."

"What people?" I ask, a little confused. My coach, standing behind Han-son, looks too happy. He holds up five fingers and makes circular motions with his hands.

"Scouts," Hanson says. Five fingers. Circular motions. Rings? As if to answer, Hanson says, "Olympic team scouts."

My skin tingles again.

"But of course, that's just between you and me," he says with a conspira-torial smirk. "Really, the big draw is the chance to show off to a crowd and help raise donation money. This year's cause is the children's hospital in Scranton."

"I would love to be there," I say, and I can see that my coach is delighted.

"Excellent," Hanson says. "I'm looking forward to seeing you perform again."

Flashing my best and sweetest smile, I shake his hand again. The oppor-tunity to perform for Olympic scouts? Today was my first chance to shine, but tomorrow... tomorrow will be amazing.

After Hanson departs, my mother and coach start talking excitedly.

"Don't worry," my coach says, as I realize I've missed most of their con-versation, "I will take her there. If she performs even *half* as well as today, she will be star."

"I will do my best," I say.

"I can't get over how you've changed," my mother beams. "Just a couple weeks ago you were so awkward. Falling, tripping, slamming into things. And now, now... now you are just amazing. When *did* this change come about?"

My coach chuckles. "It is video cameras," he says.

My cheeks flush. But he couldn't possibly know. How could he?

"The cameras?" my mother asks.

"Since she started filming herself, she's gotten better. Slow improve-ments at first, but studying those films really helps. I mean, look at how much progress she's made."

"And today?" Mother seems almost convinced.

"I love having cameras on me," I say. "Makes me feel special... like a... a hero..."

"Well, I hope you don't like it *that* much," my coach says, "or tomorrow might be problem."

"What do you mean?"

"Anderton Invitational," he says, slowly, as if that should help me decipher his meaning. "Is closed to press."

I swallow hard, trying to hide my shock. There would be cameras at the Olympics. Nationals, Regionals... all televised. I had just assumed... "No press, fine, but mom can bring–"

"No, no, no, Jillian," my coach says. "No cameras at all. Is for charity. Anderton Enterprises does not allow people to record events in their buildings. They cannot control recording, or profit from it, so they allow nothing. No exceptions. Oh, don't look so downcast. I'm sure you will perform just as well. You will be amazing."

"Sure," I say, not convinced. I shoulder my bag and turn to the exit. I feel like running and not turning back. Glancing down, I see my legs. Not bruised. All healed. And now I'm supposed to go back to the way I was? What will people think? They'll think today was a fluke – that it was my own personal fifteen minutes of fame, all spent in one glorious afternoon. A single video disc of an amazing performance, to torment me forever. Somehow, the gold medal around my neck feels a little heavier.

I *need* the cameras. Without them, I'm just an accident waiting to happen. I can't possibly perform at this event.

*Scouts*... I can't back out. It's an amazing opportunity. A stellar performance for them could propel me past the Regional team, straight onto the Olympic team. But how can I deliver such a performance without using an external view?

I catch the eye of a young girl in the crowd, sitting next to her father, watching me. I smile and she waves, blows me a kiss. Can't help but smile back as I catch the kiss, hold it close to my heart, and thank her. I feel another tingle snaking down my back. All my worries melt away. After all, I've done it, haven't I? I've acquired the admiration of a girl who I probably will never see again. Today, I'm her hero. I, and others, will watch recordings of today's performance. Whatever happens tomorrow can't take that away from me. I adjust my bag and start the long walk to the car.

*   *   *

In the morning, my coach picks me up. I wait at the end of the driveway, bag at my feet, soaking up the sunshine and enjoying the light breeze. My mother had scheduled an appointment with some doctor and wasn't going to be coming. According to my coach, they had told me that yesterday, after I had agreed to come to the Anderton Invitational. Probably the part of the conversation I had missed. I had other things on my mind. Not having her along was actually a relief. That meant if I failed, she wouldn't even find out for hours. I could wear what I liked and didn't have to listen to her fret. Plus she had a tendency to fiddle with my hair. I didn't need that annoyance today.

"We have two hours before event starts," my coach says as he puts my bag in his car. "I was thinking we should stop by studio and make sure you do not forget *correct* ending to your routine."

"Okay," I respond. I didn't want to remind him that I had done the correct ending when it counted, and had won the competition. There was no point in arguing that point or any other. I wanted to go to the studio, to practice the routine. I had other reasons on my mind.

He pulls into the parking lot and turns off the engine. "Do not worry, Jillian. You will do fine today. I just want to give you chance to warm up before we get to event."

I nod, and we exit the car. Inside the studio, I take a quick look around. Dark, quiet, serene. My coach flips on a few lights and I scan the seats around the perimeter. No cameras. I hadn't brought mine, and nobody had abandoned theirs. Good. I need to prove that I had earned the medal yesterday. Or, at least, I need to know that I hadn't.

After stretching, I start my floor exercise. At least there's no equipment for me to trip over. My coach watches in silence as I perform my routine. I take it a little slower than usual, but he doesn't say anything. I get halfway through the routine without incident, then scuff my foot on the mat and almost slip. Faltering for but a moment, I twist and recover. I catch a glimpse of my coach's face and he doesn't look upset. Not entirely pleased, but not upset either. Sort of a familiar middle ground with him. When I finish the routine (with the proper ending), he slowly nods his head.

"Again," he says.

And I do it again. Slightly worse this time. I misjudge the timing on one of my jumps and fall.

"Again," he repeats as I rise from the mat. "From top."

On my third attempt, I have fewer problems, but it's still not perfect. He tells me to control my breathing, to concentrate. I *am* concentrating, but not on the routine. I'm upset with myself. I've become dependent on the cameras. I can't perform well without that third-person view. In fact, I'm actually *worse* now than I was before. While thinking of this, I scuff my foot again and fall.

"Again."

I move to the starting position and start the routine again, from the top, and give the absolute worst performance I have ever given since I first learned this routine. I leap into the air for the first jump, misjudge the landing, and slam into the mat.

"Again."

I rise up, ready to start over again. My coach's watch plays a light tune and he announces that it's time to go. I grab my jacket and follow him to the car.

We drive to the other side of town in silence. I stare out the window, inhaling the recycled air with short breaths. While stopped at a red light near a fast food place, I connect to their network and send a message to Alice. She responds instantly with her usual concern. Before I can reply, we're through the intersection. I watch the town fly past the window. It looks different to me now. It's not just fast food joints (that I can't eat at) and media stores (that I don't have time to shop at). There are trees and birds and, in the distance, a group of old buildings covered in peeling paint and graffiti. We pass a park that I've never seen before. There are kids there, my age and younger, and they are just playing. I can't remember the last time I was allowed to do that. I'm not sure I could remember how. A moment later we are past it, and I'm watching a small strip of stores go past, with a lonely car at the far end of the parking lot. The buildings are new, covered in solar panels and corporate logos. When did this little town of ours get so big? What else have I missed?

The car pulls into a parking lot and I turn to see where we are. The Anderton building is a huge mountain of steel and plastic. It looks big enough to comfortably fit the entire stadium we were in yesterday. I follow my coach into the building, where he announces my name and signs me in. I can hear an edge in his voice and I know what it is. Disappointment. I've come full circle, and we both know it. He probably thinks yesterday was a fluke. My fifteen minutes of fame. I know I can perform better, but I need the external view. I *need* the cameras. My eyes start to tear up as I come to this realization.

Turning my head to wipe them, I see a camera mounted on the ceiling, slowly turning on its base as it scans the entryway. I look through the double doors beneath it and into the arena. Beyond the other gymnasts, I can see another camera, mounted against the opposite wall, looking right back at me.

*Security* cameras. My heart sinks.

Security *cameras*. My hopes rise.

How much security could a sports arena possibly have? Still, I'm not a trained hacker, I'm a gymnast, and a rather poor one at that. If they have any security at all, or if anyone is monitoring the network, they'll find me immediately. What would they do to a sixteen-year-old girl? My career would be over, for one thing. My coach would probably stop training me, which might be a blessing if I can't be the gymnast I want to be anyway. I can deal with the parental disappointment (I've had so much practice there).

Ahead, I see Mister Hanson. He recognizes me, and his smile widens. I see him turn toward the crowd and make a gesture, trying to get someone's attention. I follow his gaze and see a group of men with small tablets on their knees. They regard me with interest and talk amongst themselves. The scouts.

"You look nice today," my mother says.

"Mom?" I whirl and stare at her.

"The doctor was able to take me early," she says. "Are you ready Jilly? Big day today. Everything rides on your performance. I couldn't miss out on seeing this."

My body shakes. I take a deep breath to calm my nerves. I realize in a moment that I've been given the toughest choice of my life – compete as I am, and my career is probably over; or connect to the security cameras and hope to God that they aren't being monitored adequately. If I don't use the cameras, or if I'm caught trying to use them, my career is over. There's only one way I can win. I have to use the cameras. And I have to do it without getting caught.

I close my eyes and log into the arena's wireless network. Surveillance Pro provides a list of twenty cameras that it finds nearby. While staring at the list, I get another message from Alice, responding to my earlier note about the morning's practice. I tell her about the cameras. Suddenly both eyes blank out and all I can see is her face.

"Do not do it," she says. "Jill, you cannot even consider that. This is an Anderton facility. *Anderton*. They have very good security."

*Alice, I have to*, I think.

"We have been through a lot together," she begins, then starts to talk so fast that I can't make out the words any more. My mother is also saying something, something about my eyes. Both voices echo and intertwine, making me feel dizzy. I shake my head to clear my vision but Alice's face is still there, everywhere I turn.

"Alice, please, stop," I say.

"Alice?" my mom says. Alice's voice halts and I hear my mom continue. "Now there's a name I haven't heard in a long time. You can't still be playing with her, honey. Not the same Alice, at least. I thought your father threw her out years ago."

"Who is Alice?" my coach asks. "Friend? I have not met."

The dizziness intensifies. I feel like I should sit, but my vision is still overridden by Alice's concerned face.

"Oh, she's just one of those artificial friend robots," my mother replies. "One of the older models. We bought her for Jill's sixth birthday."

"Is nice gift," my coach says, sounding more pleasant than usual.

"Well, we certainly thought so. But I was sure Edward threw her out a few years ago."

"I saved her," I say, remembering the day. Alice's internal battery had died, the warranty had expired, and my father was going to throw her out. I managed to break through the skull casing and rescue her memory card. Uploading her consciousness to my computer was an easy job, and I got to keep her as my friend. My best friend. My only friend. At some point, she figured out how to escape into the Internet, yet she still kept in touch. We still shared everything with each other.

*Alice, please go, I need to compete soon,* I think.

Alice stares at me for a few moments, then smiles. "Of course," she says. "I look forward to your performance."

She vanishes, letting the room come into focus again. I close my eyes, desperately trying to ignore my mother's continued conversation with my coach. I know I'm not in the right mindset to perform today, so I need to motivate myself. In my head, I flip through some menus and play a copy of yesterday's performance. My shining moment. The best performance I've ever given. I would always have this moment and this video to cherish. What happened today didn't really matter. Perhaps in a few years I'd be showing this video to my daughter–

Doing exactly the same thing to her that my mom did to me? Maybe I could make her wear the same leotard that I wore in this video. Maybe she'll grow to hate it as much as I hate my mother's green one. Perhaps she'll waste desperate hours trying to destroy the garment? No, I don't want to be like that. For years I've been training as a gymnast, and for what? So I could relive *her* days of glory?

As I see myself perform the floor exercise, I realize that I've seen this before. The routine that I've been doing is hers. The motions I make in my video are the same ones she made in the video she keeps watching. The video she keeps making me watch. The music is the same too. I can't believe how I didn't realize that before.

Maybe, today, I *should* fail.

# LAST DEFENDER
## BY SHELLI-JO PELLETIER

I t was said that mankind had forgotten the ancient arts.

The tour guides said it, leading their flocks like a mother duck with a procession of young through the *Lady*'s interior, while he crouched above in the shadows of the arched ceiling. He had heard all their speeches before. How the humans had lost the knowledge to construct the grand cathedrals, gone to the ages of time. How the immense walls of *Our Lady* were constructed with the use of simple wooden nails, a fact that seemed to astound many. How they talked of the small, saintly chapel only a block away: a structure where the stone masonry was nothing more than a thin framework supporting walls made entirely of stained glass. The knowledge to build such things, they said, was an art lost to the minds of men.

So too had the art been lost that kept him prisoner here, he supposed. For in his many years within these walls, he had seen all of his brethren turned to dust or empty husks, ceasing to rise from their stone sleep, one by one. There was now nothing left of them but a monument – a mockery of what was once a living creature. Though he couldn't travel beyond the grounds of the old cathedral, he could see across the *Seine*, beyond the streets of glowing lights, to others like himself perched on rooftops and gutters, spewing water when it rained. None of those that he could see displayed any evidence of remaining life, if they ever had it at all and were not just replicas carved by human hands. He feared he was the last.

Once man had spoken of him with fear. In the wild days of his youth, hooting and hollering from the bell tower alongside his brothers, they would frighten the humans, sending them scuttling from the church to the safety of their homes, reminding them of danger and darkness that waited for them be-yond the edge of their torchlight.

The men of Paris used to speak of him with fear, now they spoke of him as architecture. And he was no longer interested in scaring churchgoers, only in doing his duty.

The gargoyles had always been protectors. It was their nature. They pro-tected their dens, their land, and each other. Mankind knew this, carved their likeness into waterspouts and awnings, hoping to trick creatures of evil into avoiding the area and at the same time trick their churchgoers into more holy behavior. The leering visage of a gargoyle frightened a human as much as it offered him protection.

But for their most precious structures, those men who knew the ancient arts had not been satisfied with mere likenesses.

He didn't remember how he had been captured. He remembered being young, carefree, and foolish. Occasionally, he remembered a halo of light and searing pain and a sense of loss; but most often, he left the memories to gather dust in the corner of his mind. He and his kind had been put here to protect the grand edifice from the spirits of darkness. Their own will mat-tered not; the humans had known the old words that would bind a gargoyle to stone and wood and foundation for as long as he drew waking breath. The gargoyles became protectors of the sacred churches for all time, defending against any evil that might come upon them. Standing guard against the ones who lived in darkness, who loved to taint the innocent, to rob the weak of fealty and faith.

\*   \*   \*

These days he thrived on routine. Though most days he slept in his shell of stone, he still knew the time that the three arched wooden doors on the west front of the building would be unlocked each morning, when the nuns would light the rows and rows of candles to cast illumination in the *Lady*'s dim interior, and when the tourists would come flocking in, cooing and ruffling their feathers like the pigeons roosting in the eaves.

Before all that, the rising of the morning sun might quicken the sluggish blood in his frozen veins. Unyielding skin would give way to thick flesh, lungs would draw in their first breath of air, toes would curl and tail would twitch, and then his horned head would turn to regard the old balustrade on which he stood. Unlike the stone mockeries perched around him, those who would be only stone until the day they crumbled, he could still move himself between one form and the next. He sometimes dozed for weeks, or months. But always a hint of danger would awaken him, reminding him that he was still a prisoner, still the last guardian who prowled *Our Lady*'s halls. Such it must be now.

He vaguely wondered what it could be, stretching his wings out to catch the earliest rays of the glowing sun. Something had awakened him. Something itched just under his reanimated skin. He pivoted on one muscular arm, swung himself down from the low stone wall, and disappeared into the northern tower.

Making his rounds was an old habit now. He had a usual perch, and if one day out of fifty he was not seen there, it raised no alarms among the humans as far as he was aware. The humans only saw what they wanted to see. Looking up from the street so far below, perhaps they told themselves it was

a trick of shadow and light that one of the stone statues appeared to be missing. Or that it had been removed by the caretakers to repair damage from the
elements. It would always reappear before long, after all.

Though he had a barrel chest and thick, rippling arms to carry himself
around the building, and a short tail as supple as rope which trailed behind,
only long practice saved him from an awkward and unbalanced gait. His hind
limbs, which he remembered with only a phantom pain now and again, had
been taken from him by the same spell which sealed his fate as the perma-
nent protector of *Our Lady*. He now moved with a loping gait by swinging
his compact body forward and carrying himself along with his arms, instinct
after centuries of practice.

He passed under the four bells of the north tower and slipped down the
spiral stone staircase inside, steps worn smooth by a hundred tourists each
day, down to the interior of the cathedral, a single vast open room in the
shape of a cross, like so many built in the age the *Lady* was constructed.
Here, it was a world of perpetual gloom, where the only lights came from the
dim electric torches on the walls, the rows of candles lit in honor of the
Mother, and the bright colors pooling on the stone floor from the sunlight
striking the great glass windows. In the high heat of summer, the dim and
cool within the walls were welcome relief. And the sprawling ceiling so far
overhead, where the lights could not reach, promised to hide him from wandering eyes as long as he kept away from the tour groups and hid his movements in the shadows.

The great portals at the west end of the building made a dragging sound
as the locking bolt slid free. He froze on his perch, the lip of a stone arch
stretching across the ceiling. One of the doors opened only wide enough to
admit two figures in black habits, and the gargoyle relaxed as the door closed
and was locked once again.

Whether the old nuns knew of his existence or not, he couldn't say or
come to care. Truthfully he found it hard to tell one human from another,
they looked so alike. Even more so when they all wore the trappings of their
calling. Regardless, he was less wary of being sighted by them than the noisy
tourists with their searching, eager eyes. The nuns glided across the stone

floor almost as silent as himself, and never minded a stray noise or comment-ed on a moving shadow.

As the nuns lit the lines of candles on the tables by the doors, and set the locked collection boxes in their proper places, he continued on his way across the ceiling, to search for what disturbance had awoken him. He heard them talking in low voices, calling each other by old names. *Maria. Marthe.* Names he had heard time and again over the centuries.

He knew at one point in the past he had had a name himself. When others of his kind had roamed within the walls with him, they had ways of telling each other apart. But time had taken it from him. He didn't often remember their names, or his own. Sometimes glimpses of his past returned to him. Now, as the nuns murmured down below, he recalled one old friend who had scales like a fish and a particular bend in his beak. They had all had a good laugh at his expense when a sparrow decided the space between his horns would make a fine nesting site. But that was so long ago, and now there was little amusement to be found. In the place where Bentbeak had once perched now sat a carved replica with a woebegone expression, quite unlike the cheerful fellow's true countenance.

It didn't matter much at this point. He didn't need a name, for no one knew he existed. There was no one who remembered the old arts, and no one who remembered he was here to call him by name, so it seemed fitting to cast it out of his mind centuries ago. When he thought of himself at all, he called himself "The Last."

*Our Lady* was built to be a grand structure, rising high above everything else in the city, the two square bell towers on the west front an imposing con-trast to the small but fragrant garden surrounding the east end. He could tell it was high summer now; the sun was harsh and the flowers were in bloom, leaving this end of the cathedral in a swath of fragrant bouquet. He had left the cathedral's interior and now cast his eyes over the garden, but all seemed to be at peace down below among the flowering bushes and trees.

Taking a moment to perch on one of the flying buttresses on the side of the structure, he coiled his squat, muscular body on the cool stone that was already warming in the light of the rising sun.

He raised his round snout to sniff the air, trying to detect a figure born from darkness, but only the smell of chocolate crepes and oil paints drifted up from the land below, the artists and vendors of the streets spread out along the banks of the *Seine*. His roving eyes took in all there was to see. The *Lady* stood tall and strong on the eastern end of an island in the middle of the great river. Small bridges allowed the humans and their growling carriages to cross to and fro on either side. What had once been a surging impediment that sep-arated the sprawling city of Paris was now laced with bridges like a lady's garment, all up and down the banks. On either side of the island the city raced away to the horizon and beyond, the *Seine* a black cut slicing through the rows of streets and soot-darkened buildings. Like a beacon of light, *Our Lady* stood above the land, and when the gargoyle perched on the top of the towers he could look down upon everything.

The darkness that had woken him seemed to be gone now. Perhaps it was only a spirit passing through the atmosphere overhead or a shudder from the end of the world, rippling back through time. Such things were not unknown to him. In time, it would reveal itself and he would know it, but for now his search had tired him and he wished only to return to his usual perch before the streets filled with more than just early morning patrons. Already he dreaded the prattle of the tour guides intruding on his gray dreams. Silently, he slipped into the shadows under the flying buttress, crossing the length of the building back to the western towers.

*   *   *

When night fell the gargoyle awoke again, a growl of agitation on thick lips. The air felt off. Something more insistent than before had dragged him from stone sleep to waking flesh and blood.

*Our Lady* was a different creature at night. Her colors were gone with no sunlight to sweep the reds and greens of the stained glass across the stone floor. She stood silent and empty, locked to the public after the tourists had left. The Father had finished mass and sent his sheep home, and the nuns had gathered the collection boxes on their way out. The air inside her grew cold and still, like stone.

Humans had mastered the darkness now. To combat their fear of what lurked beyond their sight, they lit up all of Paris with the coming of each night. The streets trailed globes of golden radiance, and even the exterior of the *Lady* was dotted with illumination. For him, it only meant starker shadows to hide in.

An urge to find the source for this unease prickled through his senses, so the bulky beast left the balustrade and glided along the flying buttresses, moving with the ease and grace of long familiarity, knowing that the darkness and these stone arches that ran down the sides of the cathedral like a rib cage blocked any view from a night wanderer on the street far below.

He stopped and surveyed the eastern garden for the second time in recent memory, but this time he hardly had to pause before he recoiled from the harsh, astonishing stench of a Daemicus.

From times before the written word, the Daemicus and their dark brethren stalked mankind and all other living beings, jealous of the life that quickened through their pulsing veins. All but forgotten by man now, the gargoyle nevertheless remembered. They had been the fiercest and most challenging of all foes when the gargoyles were plentiful upon the earth. Although it had been a century since he had last battled one, he would not underestimate this presence now. He would never forget these agents of darkness who yearned to pull mankind down into the depths of despair. He could never forget that this was the reason his kind had been captured and coerced to defend man's most precious structures so long ago.

And now a Daemicus polluted his garden.

Though many years had passed, he had not forgotten that they could hardly be seen by the naked eye. Practically formless, even in broad daylight they could slip from shadow to shadow, and the humans would go about their daily lives noticing nothing but a flicker in the corner of their eyes, easily dismissed as a pennant waving in the wind or the reflection of sunlight off a metal awning's frame.

But it was the smell that always identified them. His snout had wrinkled the moment the sweet, sick, oil-slick scent wafted up to him. Immediately his wings spread and mantled like an agitated hawk, and he turned a sharp eye down to the grassy nook below, though there was nothing to see but shades and shadow. He looked nonetheless, and inhaled sharply to taste the air.

"Ah," a dank voice said immediately, "so here you are, the last."

The gargoyle's horned head swung down in surprise, for a Daemicus was cruel and clever, but he had never heard one speak in such formal, measured tones, almost polite in its introduction. Under heavy brows his eyes narrowed in concentration, but all he could see was a flicker in a bush that might have been a songbird settling its wings for the night.

It was a very old Daemicus, he could tell. His round, ape-like ears could discern a slight creaking in the garden below, which could have been a thick tree branch swaying in the wind, though he knew it to be the creaking parts of a dark, ancient being. And the smell was particularly strong.

"For surely, you are the last," the voice added suddenly, as if it had not paused to listen for his reaction at all. "I came all this way, to the heart of Paris, to see the last gargoyle. Your promptness is so refreshing."

He strengthened his heart against a tide of sorrow. He had no reason to expect the Daemicus to speak the truth. Indeed, he knew it would have said anything if it could cause pain or despair. But of course, the deepest despair always came from truth, and if such an ancient enemy really had traveled for so long and still called him the last...

The silence down in the garden was not the high tension of a creature waiting for a response, but a calm sickening patience of one who knew that they had struck home.

"Yes, you're something of a legend around my people," hissed the Daemicus. *Creek creek* as it adjusted its position. "They speak of you. The last living protector of the *Lady*. I wondered if you were just a legend and nothing more, so I came to see."

The gargoyle didn't respond.

There was a brief cackle of laughter then, a sound like the *Seine* vomiting up nails upon its concrete banks. And then, perhaps its evil mission complete for now, he heard a scampering sound as it slipped out of the garden and fled down the street. When the stink of it faded too, he knew it was gone.

*    *    *

It came back the next night.

The gargoyle was already perched on the eastern end of the rooftop when he heard the creak of its ancient form slithering across the cobblestones that ran just beyond the line of garden trees. Unheeding, it pooled like liquid ink between two flowering bushes and sniffed along the stately building's masonry, like a dog investigating a neighbor's garden once it slipped the fence. The gargoyle snapped his bulldog jaws, fanned his wings to warn the Daemicus off, but it ignored him until it stiffened, a hound scenting prey.

A cackle of delight came from the shadows in the garden below. Suddenly, a fluttering of wings exploded through the enclosed grassy space. Two pigeons, a mated pair, burst out from under a bush where the flickering shadow coiled. The Daemicus made no attempt to catch them. Peering down, the gargoyle could see the gleam of streetlight reflecting off the curve of talons suspended above a small nest. Pale round shapes sat in the little cup of dried grass and twigs.

"Ahh," said the Daemicus, as if savoring a bouquet, as it cast a sickly yellow look upward at the gargoyle perched on the wall above. "Such innocence begs to be plucked, I think," it said. "Don't you agree, old one? After all these years, don't you yearn to be the cause of some disruption? Oh no, but you are under a geas which says you must protect *any* within the walls. How terribly inconvenient that must be." It made as if to clench its claws around the nest.

The gargoyle readied his wings and launched himself from the wall. Wind whistled by his snout and ears as he plummeted to earth, his heavy body pulling him down like a hurtled stone. Leathery wings snapped open to stop his fierce descent.

He angled his glide to keep him close to the *Lady*'s wall, knowing the ancient arts would react if he passed too close to the edge of his allotted territory. In his youth, many times he had felt the power of the fiery hand reaching out to one of his brethren as they tried to leave the chapel grounds, like spider web tendrils wrapping around their bodies, all silk and suffering. And then there would be a scorched smell like burnt flesh, and nothing but dust particles floating on the wind.

With wings open to guide his fall, he raised both arms as he swooped over the Daemicus. Each hand tipped with five diamond-like shards dug into the shadow as he passed over, a feeling like cool breath running between his fingers. The Daemicus let out a screech of pain and dodged to one side, taking refuge in the street, beyond the gargoyle's reach.

He turned his swoop back into a climb, trading speed for height as he soared back up to his original perch and cast a meaningful look down on the dark being.

"Ah, you're still quick for such an elder!" hissed the creature, who the gargoyle was sure was just as old as he – if not older – and yet moved with the same nimble grace. He didn't bother to deign to a reply.

Wary now, the Daemicus flowed around the edges of the garden, taunting the gargoyle by staying just beyond the *Lady*'s grounds. "Such a shame!" it chuckled. "Such a shame, that a creature so devoted to his duty would give so much, and yet be required to give still more. So long has he been here. How many centuries? Wouldn't it be grand if the old arts were to be broken someday and he were free to choose his own duty? Oh wouldn't *that* be something..."

The gargoyle settled his weight, coiling his tail until he could rest his legless lower body on it, tipping his short neck to keep his attention focused on the courtyard. A trio of humans appeared from the shadows between the lampposts, laughing and teetering as they made their way down the sidewalk toward the nearest bridge. Neither the gargoyle nor the Daemicus moved, but the gargoyle tracked them with his eyes, looking for the small silver cylinders that were common ammunition for those who defaced stone buildings. When they were gone he looked back to the spot in the garden where the dark creature had been flickering, but now the grass was empty. He flared his nostrils; the scent was dissipating into the night.

The gargoyle didn't believe such an old one would give up so easily. He prepared to stand guard above the garden throughout the night.

*   *   *

A shrill scream, sensed rather than heard, rocketed him from stone to flesh so fast his body burned along every vein. Bright sunlight streamed across his senses, for a moment blinding him.

Rot and ruin! It was in the bell tower! The fool would force him to respond in the full light of day! The gargoyle launched himself from the wall about the eastern garden. He swooped along the flying buttresses that stretched alongside the building, swinging under each stone arch with his muscular arms and using his wings to glide to the next, in full view of any human below who might be taking in the *Lady*'s architecture. He could only hope that the simple creatures would continue to be oblivious to anything they did not want to see. To them he could be nothing but a large pigeon flying under the buttresses to roost, or the reflection of a flying machine streaking across the stained glass.

The shrill cry of a human child reached his ears as he flew into the southern tower and laid eyes on the Daemicus in corporeal form, all slithering scales and fur and fang. It was tangled around a small human as it dragged it across the stones, under the great bell, *Emmanuel*, toward the edge of the tower. Obviously it planned to throw the child over the edge to the cobblestones far below.

Where had it come from? There were no tours of the towers this day, the gargoyle had already spotted the barricade on the street below that was put up to block admittance on days the towers needed cleaning or repair. Perhaps the child had grown bored listening to the sermons of the mass, or perhaps it had simply had the bad luck to stray from its touring family when the Daemicus had returned to the *Lady*.

The gargoyle drew a breath as he landed on the floor of the stone belfry, expanding his barrel chest before letting loose a scream the likes of which hadn't been heard within the walls of *Our Lady* for over a hundred years, since the last Daemicus had dared to scale the walls of the sacred building. *Emmanuel* cupped his cry and amplified it, the old bell ringing with the furious sound until it echoed again and again through the tower.

The ancient one recoiled in pain from the sound, its claws clamped over its ears. In the next moment it retaliated by grabbing the small human and raising a taloned hand above its head, too old and strong to be stopped by such fleeting measures. In one moment it could swipe downward, parting head from shoulders like a bird would pluck a seed from a bush. The gargoyle could see its claws and fangs were dripping red, though the child appeared whole for now. He could not guess at what horrors the Daemicus had been up to on the streets of Paris before returning this day.

At that moment a sudden sound entered the bell tower, the echoing flutter of pigeon wings, as a mated pair streaked through the belfry. Only for an instant the Daemicus was distracted, pale sickly eyes darting upward, but it was enough. In that instant the gargoyle struck.

They rolled across the tower floor, the shrieks of the gargoyle's deep throat merging with the shrill cries of the human child and the furious howls of the Daemicus. With a swipe of his tail that was half luck, the gargoyle knocked the human child back, out of the Daemicus's reach. But with that opening, the dark creature swung its sinuous body and slammed into him with powerful hind legs, throwing him across the tower, out from under *Emmanuel* to slam up against the wall with a crack that the gargoyle more felt than heard.

In pain, he scrambled to his feet, knowing he had to remain a threat to the ancient creature or it would return its attention to the child. But the Daemicus's focus was solely on him. It slithered rapidly across the floor, the fetid odor of its body wafting up under the bell, twining around the clapper. "Let me throw it!" it hissed to the gargoyle, malevolent eyes flashing. "How could you care!? You hate these creatures. They have imprisoned you for centuries. You owe them nothing! Let me throw it." Its voice dropped until the words pooled out of its throat like hot candle wax, and the gargoyle circled around the circumference of the tower warily, keeping his distance. "*Perhaps* if you fail in your duty, the spell will be broken and you will be free. Did that never occur to you, old one? Its power has waned over so many years, and no human now remembers how to renew it. Let me throw it!"

The gargoyle looked past the Daemicus, at the coin of the sun in the brilliant sky. He heard the sounds of vice and vagabonds from the Paris streets below. He heard the faint scrambling of little feet on the steps behind him, and the furious snarl of the Daemicus as it too noticed its prey fleeing.

His body was already tiring. He would lose in a drawn-out fight. Such an old and powerful enemy before him, its age and intelligence had been used to bring evil upon the world for countless years. The gargoyle knew his duty, knew any one of his kind would do whatever was necessary to stop such a thing.

He coiled his tail and rushed at the Daemicus, thrusting with muscled forelimbs and spreading his wings wide as his ponderous bulk struck the dark creature squarely, this sinuous form not nearly as nimble as a patch of oily shadow. The gargoyle's momentum launched them both over the railing, past the woebegone mockery that perched on the balustrade, in full view of the humans hurrying in and out of the great arched doorways in the courtyard below. The gargoyle closed his eyes. Like a rock they struck the surface of the *Seine*.

No fiery hand, nothing of the ancient arts, took his body to dust as he passed beyond the grounds of the church.

The gargoyle opened his eyes. The Daemicus's body floated before him, dazed, like an oil slick on the water's surface. But his own squat body began to sink immediately. Like the stone they could embody, his kind could not swim or stay buoyant. He knew he would be dragged down, his lungs would fill with water, his flesh become cold and lifeless, and the Daemicus would be free. Unless–

The ancient being roused itself as it felt bands of iron, tail and forelimbs, wrap around its scaly body. Even as it began to thrash, panicked, it gave a hissing laugh. "All this time!?" it said, choking on water lapping around its snout. "All this time, you were free! How long? How long did you know you were no longer held by the ancient arts?!"

The gargoyle didn't answer, but curled his broad torso tighter around the creature while its struggles grew more frantic. And as he hardened his body to stone, sending himself deeply asleep, sinking down to the bottom of the *Seine* with the Daemicus in his embrace, he could just hear its scream of frustration, with water rushing into its corporeal body.

"*Why–?!*"

But the gargoyle said nothing.

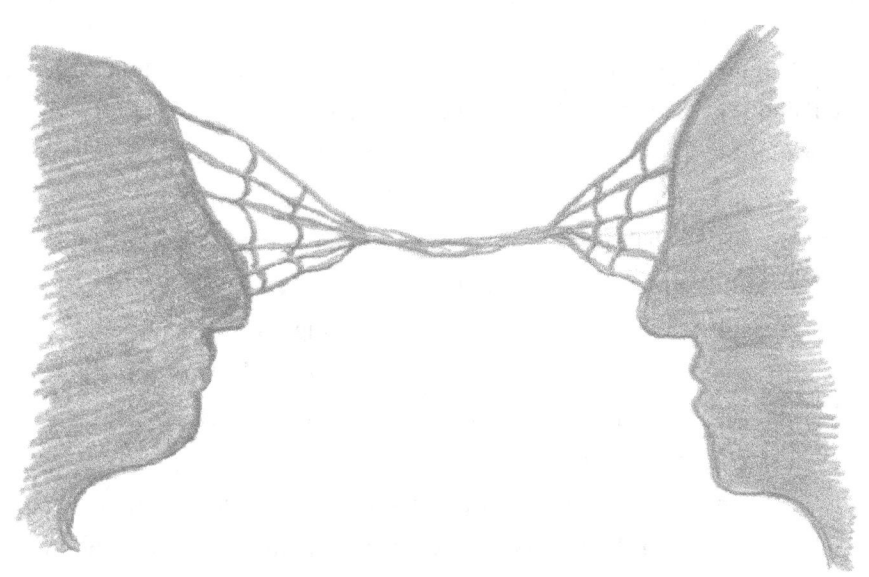

# DISRUPTION
## BY D.L. HARVEY

### 1

Braven Clair stumbled into the space port. He didn't know why he had to disappear, and yet it was all he knew. He felt he should be someone more than he was in that moment, but with the drug running through him, he could make sense of very little. The quick and erratic pulse wracked his ears in competition with the ruckus of the crowd's garbling. The worst of his sensory disorientation was the searing pain slicing at his eyes, forcing him to keep them heavy lidded and almost blind. He knew he had been poisoned, and that knowledge drove him to run and hide. He pulled his jacket more tightly around him and kept moving forward.

He could still see shadowed and lit areas. The overhead lights glared, twisted, and fell from the ceilings and corners then bounced off of the shined metal or glassed walls of corridors. A band of video screen that lined the upper walls that constantly cycled news added its large array of colors and noise to an already chaotic environment. He vaguely remembered that the cycler would guide him to the ships' docks. He steered toward the shadows, denying himself from the indulgence of enchanting dancing rainbows made by the mixture of passing people, bent light, and reflective surfaces. His years of dance lessons from childhood gave him a measure of control over his balance and stride as his sight went in and out of focus.

It had taken a while before he grasped what the lady in the window wanted. He'd grunted when he handed his wallet for payment. Without thinking, he'd gone straight to a port that would take him through space to another planet. In a brief moment, he realized what he was doing, traveling somewhere, other than on Pater-Rio, and he felt safer.

He hadn't heard the cost of the ticket or the name of the ship. He flipped his ticket into view; the images and symbols slid into one another with every movement. He saw something that looked like the dock number, 18, but he couldn't be sure. A shift of his hands revealed the pilot he sought, a woman with a hood to hide her hair as it emphasized her face. In this light, she'd have tanned skin and large, tilted eyes. She wore a jacket of a dark, muddy green with a lot of pockets. But the lights kept shining on the flexible ticket distorting names and other words he needed. He knew he'd have no trouble seeing it any other time, but right then, it kept weaving, tilting, glinting, glaring, falling and rising. It made his eyes tear.

His muscles shook with the toll he was taking on them by the time he tried to hand his ticket to a hawker. The hawker tried to dodge him but with a lithe side-step he was able to loom over the little person. He tried to close the space between their faces so he could get a good look at the features. They were dark complexioned with high cheekbones. Were they male or female?

The voice was male. And he kept trying to back up. "Sorry, man, that's not me. I'm booked up." The hawker pointed further down the rounding corridor, "That ship arrived not long ago; down that a'ways."

With the lights so blurry, he was surprised to see a person when he sighted down the corridor, following the direction of that pointed finger. She seemed to shine even brighter than the lights and the people passing by her.

"Good luck with her, man," the hawker volunteered with a chuckled mocking underlying his words, "she's going to lay you out flat."

Braven caught those muttered words as he turned away when other sounds receded like a tide, giving him a break in the audio torture. He was further surprised when another break in the waves of overwhelming noise receded for a moment again. It allowed him to hear the high, shrill, whining voice as a bloated woman passed near him, "She turned off everything." A muscled guard that had accompanied the annoying woman shouldered Braven out of their space calling him, "drugged scum," just before the return of the crashing vortex of volume. There was no longer a distinction of origination of sounds.

His focus on the brightly shining person helped him continue toward her. The shapely petite body, his destination, emitted a halo of lights that were yellow at the end, but were darker at the shimmering base. A coalescing, dark red light wove through her body's shining rays and swirled around her as if caressing. He grunted appreciation of her curvy little body. Then, she seemed to be floating toward him, gaining height until she was an arm's-length away. He held out her ticket. She must be his dock. When she reached out to receive his ticket, silver lightning struck out from her forehead and then he was out.

## 2

He knew he was awake and his eyes narrowed to slits against the glare of the sun on the horizon. The glowing woman was far away talking to a mannish person on a hover-chair, that was suspended more than possible above the ground, as it lacked the use of a propeller. The distance made it easier for him to observe. A classically scenic sunset/rise cast a gorgeous, gentle, mustard glow on desert-like rolling hill before him, but it burned.

Evidence arose forcing him to realize and to accept three things. First, the mustard sunset, dry winds, and odd smells indicated that he was neither on the docking station nor on Pater-Rio. Second, to Braven's mind's eyes, the woman still glowed and they were still connected. The silver line that had initially hit him from her forehead was doing more than just connecting them. It seemed to web out, anchoring from multiple points on her body, thinning to a few separate strands that anchored at corresponding points on his. He plucked at fibers but he felt nothing within the reach of his fingertips. The image of the web was superimposed on his view of reality. The fibers shimmered with soft, pastel colors corresponding to his response to the way the woman moved. He closed his eyes to wonder at the beauty of those shim-mering colors and to what the webbing might be trying to tell him about that moment. Then, he accepted his third realization: his body resisted movement, vehemently.

He thought he'd only closed his eyes a moment but corrected that percep-tion when he was startled into opening them again. There, inches from his face, were eyes familiar from a photo drawn from his fuzzy memory. She was forcing him to meet her copper gaze of worry and resolution. She had hovered over him to wake him.

He smiled at her, and the glowing lady became solid, just a handspan away. "Hi, I'm Braven Clair. It's nice to meet you," he said.

"Well, that's good," she answered back. "You're garbled but trying to ar-ticulate." He was disappointed when her hands hovered over his body and then pulled back. He smiled. "I like you," he said, noting that the webbing was giving him information about her, what she was feeling and wanting to do in that moment. It was so confusing when his mind was pulled toward a sweet, contented, happy place and she was funneling in her tension, scrutiny, and self-censored lustiness.

The woman lifted one of those dark-brown and orange eyebrows as if to mock him. "Well, that was clear." She ran a machine over his skin and spoke while changing the settings and reading the results. "Let's see how coherent." Then, she slowed her speech and repeated information, he was certain was important, in the three languages, "I'm Cassie, Cassie Wiche... You... poi-soned... affecting your nervous system... brought you to the specialists on

Julius; K... ius... town." He was realizing he could only catch and understand pieces when she stared at his eyes so hard it hurt the back of his head.

"Yeah, the toxin is still restructuring your neurons. You'll be lucky to remember my name," she muttered, "but don't say I didn't follow the law in terms of disclosure." This he understood as if she were speaking directly into his brain.

She spoke into the device but he couldn't seem to follow closely. "Recognize: I, Cassie... pilot to the Rainbow Steed... medical care... ticket GHI-195-8588. Submit." She pressed the button and then put the machine into a sealed plastic case.

His instincts made him seek to struggle; struggle to function, to move, to respond to his commands. If he knew one thing about himself, incompetence and powerlessness were foreign experiences for him. Something wasn't right beyond that he was poisoned. He had a glimmer of self-awareness; it included panic and self-doubt. He couldn't do anything about it. The more he tried to listen, the more sounds blended. If he opened his eyes, the web glowed brighter, when she was near. And when she wasn't, light decimated him with pain.

Time was an awful companion, it existed without reference. He'd close his eyes and he'd feel the weight of it dragging him further into darkness. The oblivion was daunting, stifling, and disorienting. He'd swear he only blinked and yet, he was someplace new. So much more than the passage of time, the darkness reminded him he was helpless. There was too much he didn't know about what was happening to him, whether it was still happening, or where he was and what he could do to improve his circumstances. Time passed and he remained.

He saw clear, molten golden sky as the board he was on seemed to float. The extra sense everyone had that could locate the source of movement detected a steady thrum originating from his "bed." It swayed just slightly as wind billowed around him.

She hovered near, going in and out of his peripheral vision until they entered a cave from which he could smell water. Holes were next to stalactites in the rocky, mud covered ceiling. When the light was a dim white light in blackness, he could smell the green life of plants and still his eyes couldn't relax enough to open fully. The fragrance of the greenery filled his nose, relaxed his muscles and yet stimulated a sense of happiness as well as his worry, his survival instincts. He picked out subtle scents like fennel, a plant his family cultivated on their farm on Horto-549, but not quite like he'd ever smelled before that moment. It was as if fennel, cinnamon, clove, and maybe a little black pepper were mixed together somehow. While these smells were invigorating and intriguing in their dissimilarities from familiar spices, they were relaxing.

His arm that had moved when he had woken the first time to touch the webbing he shared with the woman refused to acknowledge his commands to reach for her again; she who had been nearby through his slippery states of awareness. The relaxing state induced by the environment seemed limited in its effect to his emotional state.

And then, he was dumped into a pond full of vines.

If his muscles hadn't been rigid, he would've struggled. The vines wrapped around his log of a body and draped around his head. He hadn't realized how much he'd come to tolerate the burning of his eyes until they were cooled under the moist, gentle pressure of the flora's attention.

Once he got past the intense fear of being the recipient of a body-dump, something no amount of chemicals could suppress, he found his reason had not abandoned him entirely. He observed and processed that he was suspended on the surface of the water. He could breathe easily. He didn't float exactly. He really should be more alarmed at the nibbles and tugs that told him something was eating his very expensive clothing as he was still physically helpless. He would bide his time and enjoy the comfort of the lassitude he felt. Reason argued that after the drugged trip, he should be grateful from his heart to the tips of each and every appendage to be alive. Then, all he could feel was gratitude. For whatever reasons he might list, he was grateful. Almost as if in response the plants warmed, hugged, and massaged his muscles. He would've purred if he could have for he had no worries impeding his gradual and complete relaxation.

# 3

"The plants really like you," Braven heard as his unconsciousness broke. The woman, whom he remembered accompanying him before his involuntary and unexplained dip into the local pond, had evidently been talking a while. She had a thick, alto voice that lilted at a pitch that was undeniably feminine, though a little rough as if from infrequent use. She'd moved to a place above his head. His gaze tried to follow the mass of long, dark and wildly curly hair that reached her lower back and earned himself an opportunity to wince and groan. His head wasn't as ready as his eyes to follow movement.

He shifted slightly as he sifted through his memory for the moment among several where she'd spoken to him to find one that included her name. He was distracted from following through with uncovering a name linked to a "K" sound by the sensation of soft and extremely, light-weight sheets. A glance told him that they were peach and that he was indeed nude. His muscles, though no longer contracted, were not yet ready for use. His brain, his mouth, his neck muscles, all seemed to have similar limitations. But thinking and swallowing worked just fine.

The smell of fennel, pepper and wood led him to believe that someone had just used or was using a wood stove to cook. He wondered if the heat he was feeling was environmental or fever. His stomach rumbled, hungry and queasy.

A dim light emitted from several points at the edges of the ceiling, diluting the orange sunbeams sifting in through a doorway with their white phosphorescence. He realized everything looked a little orange, including the woman who seemed to shy away out of his view whenever he sought her.

"Headache," he blurted, squinting against the light. He would never admit to whining. It was easy when his voice came out lighter than a whisper. With little to no ambient sound, it still sounded loud to him.

The woman had a slow sway in her walk to a far table then back to his side. Within the mug she'd retrieved from the table was some fluid; iridescent and bluer than water. He tried to focus his eyes and study the mug as it didn't move as much as the woman, who no longer glowed. Looking into the drink as it was placed beneath his nose, he resisted asking if there were floating bits in it or just bubbles. It appeared denser than most fluids.

"It's a nectar," she explained. "The Bath Plants provided it. We leave a pitcher under their roots just in case they see fit to produce any. And voila, they provided some of their rare and especially valuable nectar." He distrusted her apparent contrition when she commented, "Sorry, Remaking can leave you feeling like you've the worst hangover ever."

"Had many of those?" He caught the term "Remaking" and filed it away for later questions. He tried to catch a real look at her using his peripheral vision as he pulled her name from his subconscious depths, "K-k-case..."

The entire time she was near, his eyes had tried to track the curvy, little beauty. Then, he'd subsequently tried to shut down that train of thought, when one of her hands put the mug in his and her other helped to lift him to sitting. She kept a hand on his shoulder, supporting it but stood her arm's-length from him and gave him some space. He watched her cheeks plump as if she were smiling when he lifted the mug to his nose. It was then he saw she'd tied her hair back away from her face into a rope when she'd moved out of his line of sight. The thin fabric she was encased in was blousy and the color of the dead dirt beneath the cities' walks on Pater-Rio. He downed the drink thinking about her images shifting back and forth into clarity. She mostly looked like a light brown blob with a blackish rope dangling from her head.

"My share," she answered defiantly, redirecting his attention to the conversation and his inquiry regarding her opportunities to overindulge. "And it's Cassie." She let him drop back onto the bed indicating that he'd probably not been supporting his own weight the entire time he'd been sitting up. "Good job. I didn't think you'd remember." Then, she crossed the room, farther away from him, and leaned back against the wall near the door. "So, uhm, did you drug yourself?"

"No," offended, he'd answered too loudly and cringed. His throat felt like crinkled sandpaper. His arm ached when he pulled his hand to his eyes to massage the grit out of them.

"Do you know why someone would drug you?" Her voice sounded so distant, almost echoing and musically enticing.

"I don't know, sperm, maybe?" he fought himself from confessing his suspicions. Confusion over what he should be doing made him grimace with disappointment at himself. He felt he really shouldn't have kept any information to himself, but an older, ingrained habit had him dodging, speculating rather than answering directly.

His eyes closed of their own accord under the combined stress of use and emotional tension. His mind became overrun with a slew of remembered images; layers of blues. Among them, he had been surrounded by cobalt curtains. A blonde woman's loudly, colored mouth running down his bare chest. The soft, navy blue fabric encasing her body slid over his other extremities. His muscles flexed in memory response.

Cassie's cough pulled him back to the orange-ish bedroom. Her voice stressed, she asked, "What?" She looked to be struggling with controlling her features.

"I don't know," he answered Cassie absently while he sifted through the emerging memory. His body relived throwing that mouth off of him. The revulsion and panic of that moment with the pale woman had caused his adrenaline to kick in. He analyzed the moment from a third person point of view. Even then, he identified the sequence of events and recognized the significance of an adrenaline release. He'd deduced he was in danger, but he couldn't identify the exact indicators for thinking it.

He pulled himself back to the pertinent conversation with Cassie. He gave her a bone to chew on, "It probably has something to do with my family's company."

"So, you ran." She sounded like she was taunting him, not clarifying the situation.

He'd thrown the woman off of him. He remembered seeing her get tangled in the curtains. "God, yes," he exclaimed, heaving to sit up. He relaxed his arm by his side and tried to focus on relaxing his stomach muscles as he found out that he still couldn't sit up on his own.

"What company?"

"If you don't know, I'm not telling you." He breathed out through gritted teeth, relieved that he could still maintain some secrets. This woman was pumping him for information and he didn't know who she was, who she might work for, or if she might try to trap him herself. Then again, all of that information was available in the Interstellar Information Network (IIN). Petulant, he stared at the ceiling refusing to give her any more information.

"Fine," she backed toward the door, "be that way."

"Sorry, I should say, thank you for the rescue," he grumbled. His body started to relax into the soft bedding again.

"You have no idea," she replied. Her voice was all that was left of her in the room.

Braven regretted she left so abruptly. She had sounded too young to be entitled the level of trust necessary for him to divulge his personal information to her. She'd been suspicious of him when he should be suspicious of her. How could she possibly believe she deserved her questions answered? Why did he answer any of them? And still he wanted her to come back.

The ceiling was dirt, too. It offered no comfort. Seeking the webbing he'd imagined while delirious, he found the comfort in the connection it provided. She may not be in the room, but she remained near. After being forcibly removed from his life, a desperate escape or not, he would have to convince himself he was alone. The dirt ceiling and walls couldn't separate him from his savior; the webbing that it seemed only he could see or feel suffered no obstructions. Near or far, she was always with him, if he looked.

# 4

He used his personal IIN access-device to look up information on Cornelius, a settlement on the planet Julius. As a relatively unknown planet near ANX-321, a primary port at this end of the galaxy and sole distributor of the statis plant, Julius had very little in its entry. The population was low as it was a new settlement still under evaluation by the locals. It was a desert climate with erratic wind events for weather. Most water and life were found underground. It had a high magnetism, thought to be uninhabitable by human life and their interdependent species.

"You won't find much," Cassie informed him, interrupting his research. "And the magnetism on this planet won't let that thing last long," her hands full of clothing, gestured to his device. "Clothes for you," she set down fold-ed material of the same canvas-like texture she favored on the end of the bed.

He shut his machine down to better focus on her and their conversation, "Why am I here? How long do I need to stay?" he croaked out.

"You were poisoned. It seemed to reset your physiology; similar to what the people who live here experience. The council–"

"That man in the hover-chair?" he interrupted.

"Among them," she seemed a little surprised. "They advise observation here until you're better."

"I have responsibilities," he said more firmly. "I belong in a hospital. Pa-ter-Rio has some of the best in the quadrant. Horto-541 is probably next in line." He tried to hide his distaste for the backwater world she was showing him; hand-folded clothes that weren't washed or steamed daily and dirt floors and ceilings that could dust his foreign food.

"You'll stay here if you want to survive what that drug did to your body. That's the end of it." She walked off, her movements purposeful and unyield-ing.

In a pique, he attempted to look up information on her. His device died instead. He had been warned. He begrudgingly requested his hostess to ex-plain the environment.


# 5

Cassie started her lectures about Julius by focusing on the habitats while he followed her around in subsequent days. Above ground, the statis plant, whose reputation as a useful tool was growing in attention among the naviga-tion authority, was indigenous on Julius. It was one of few plants that could survive on the surface of bleached grains of dirt. With little surface water, the plants enjoyed a fertile but a somewhat sandy home. They lived by symbiotic relationships, the surface provided nutrition and maintained the lives of the subterranean plants, and the non-surface dwelling plants provided a nectar that could nourish most of the living organisms on the planet. The non-surface dwelling plants emerged in isolated underground terrariums, the locals called them nodes or nodules. When ANX-321 came to be known for the life-saving statis plant, Julius became a notation in the IIN.

Then she informed him of deductions the locals had made about the small planet that he found pertinently interesting. The planet seemed to reconfigure the attractions between some of the subatomic constructs. According to Cassie, the planet's high magnetism increased its gravitational pull and the sensitivity of the bioelectricity that the human body produced and had a dramatic effect on non-indigenous species. The surface plants emitted high frequency pulses that also altered the planet's non-indigenous residents. The magnetism and high pulses of sound weakened the protein bonds of cellular structures. The code that made up every single person, the DNA, was redefined, changing the human body. Not only did it kill most battery-operated devices and interfere with most surface-to-air transmissions, it killed most of the first settlers. The sub-surface plants, a treasure beneath the disguise of the barren desert, then aided in the survival of the remaining few.

The toxin introduced to his body could alter his body in a similar manner as the planet had the people. Though, his submersion had ceased the effect of the toxins and helped his body accept the changes, the process of adaptation could still kill him, too.

# 6

He eyed the clay walls of the building he had been in for a few weeks, thinking that the people lived like the plants in terrarium caves. The outdoors environment was too dry to be suffered for a long, indulgent view of open sky. He tried to stay in the kitchen as often as possible as it had the most natural light. He appreciated how the day's light shifted in colors, pale yellow in the morning, orange-ish through most of the day, and a pale muddy brown at twilight. The clean air circulated in from the outdoors into that room, too, potent with smells foreign to him, before being cycled through the rooms. The scent that wasn't quite like fennel mixed together with cinnamon and clove was strongest in the kitchen, implying that it was an atmospheric enzyme. Though he longed for the open areas, flying, running, sitting on the peaks, he was getting used to the underground lifestyle and the company.

Unused to idleness, Braven tried to help out around her home. As he walked alongside her, he couldn't believe Cassie was as tall as she was. Though he'd thought her tiny, petite, she reached his shoulders on his 6'5" person. She'd join him in towering over most of his colleagues. Her hair was massive with large curls, but it wasn't black or even dark brown; but a dark orange like so much of the landscape on Julius. Her eyes were copper in any light. And she was muscular and limber as befitting a pilot that used her body to navigate the darkwinds of space. She said she was a bodyguard to politicians in transit which, to him, meant she was a hell of a shot as well. He knew that there were biomechanical ships, but he hadn't traveled enough to have the opportunity to meet a pilot of one.

"So, how much longer do I have to stay here?" he asked. For days, he'd watched her patter around the home, he couldn't call it her home and especially not their home, cleaning. Something about having her clean up after him and serve him food bothered him. "I have responsibilities. Among them would be finding my drugger," Braven tried to sound respectful while carrying a cask she'd unearthed behind her node. They headed toward her workroom, another node not too far away.

She quirked a brow that was normally even into an arch, "Drugger?" On this day, she was outside the home, visiting different hiding places and retrieving fluid-filled containers. And she was letting him help rather than just watching while she lectured him about the world.

He'd done some heavy lifting in the form of chores when he was a kid on his parents' farm, and he was certain she should be struggling under the strain of another cask she'd hauled to the workshop. He gasped as he tried to walk and talk, "I'm not well-informed in giving titles to people who try to forcibly drug someone into–"

"Insanity?" she supplied, when they reached her workshed. She sounded fine, as if they'd taken a stroll in a garden. She started up an antique, gyrating contraption. Then, poured out measured amounts into their respective labeled containers before placing them near several different machines.

She leaned back against the dramatically moving machine to study him. When she was apt to lean, it redirected his thoughts. He was no longer interested in her projects. "Death isn't harsh enough?" he asked, leaning against the wall behind him and far away from her and the more form-fitted clothing she'd taken to wearing.

"Death was a possibility, but the drug wasn't killing you. But it was activating neurons in a pattern that promotes hallucinations, paranoia, and delusion, according to professional neurologists," she said and turned around to pour a concoction into the first machine. Then, she turned around to face him, again, and rested her hands on the level surface that reached her ribcage. She'd braced her hands on the white box vibrating her upper body when it started to do its gyrating thing again. He swore he could see her smirking, a tilt to her eyes made him think she was laughing at him.

"There are amateur neurologists," he teased. He knew he was being distracted from something. He turned his head to see a corner where cleaning supplies were haphazardly placed upon shelves. He studied it, its contents, and its contents' labels that no made sense to him.

Her voice moved around the room. He watched out of the corner of his eye as she started adding her different fluids to some other machines; some were part of the same process, while others weren't. She continued talking and her body blocked most of her movements, "There are other neurologists recording data that some of the hallucinations and delusions aren't actually hallucinations or delusions but relevant functions without training. Of course, it isn't mainstream theory, and thus, not an acceptable perspective."

He nodded, remembering his concerns were about people, his people. There were a lot of people who benefited from his business practices. He may not do every job that runs his family's multimedia conglomerate but his professional philosophy had attracted those with similar perspectives of social and ethical responsibility. Even without maximizing profits, by compromising his ethical standards, he still made enough money to make his wealth and position coveted. He couldn't give it up, not even by default. "Well, where do I fall? Who are these non-professionals keeping me here? Are they studying me? Am I just another lab rat? And what are you doing?" He turned back to her, stiff with resolve to get his life back under control.

"There aren't a lot of people on this rock, but the ones on the council agreed with my assessment; you were undergoing what we refer to as a second puberty."

He snorted, "I doubt that's what you'd call it."

"We call it Remaking. Does that term make you feel better? It's just another biological Rite of Passage. Usually, there have been hints regarding what kind of talent might be developing before the event. You're different in that you aren't from a culture with a massive amount of mental training in self-awareness to buffer the extreme hormonal fluctuations. You haven't been doing any of the physical exercises we use to keep us focused on reality; grounded, we call it. So we have to watch you." She'd circled her way around the room to finish up to stand next to the same machine she'd first turn on and let run before putting it to use.

She explained as she moved into a more comfortable position of standing, "And I'm making my ship's fuel, the fluids used to make the ice that insulates my ship from space, and I'm processing the nectar so that it can last longer and I can use it in the future, if I need to do so. I also have to adjust the cooling agents and rebuild some of the engines that maintain the environment of the ship."

Braven studied the woman as she once again lounged somewhat provocatively against the device designed to torture gelatinous materials and men alike. His brain heard her words and he'd probably be able to process them later. He stepped forward, staring at her intently and dismissing her list of non-domestic chores, "Why are you keeping me here, really?"

He sought the mental image of the web that linked them, hoping to catch some revealing thoughts or emotions. The threads had multiplied, linking more pulse points, and he could feel them increasing as he leaned closer. Her mind was going fuzzy, hazy if he was interpreting it correctly. His lips tingled in response to hers beginning to throb.

Reality showed him a face, flushed ever so slightly with muscles tightening in anger. She was biting her lips, "There are no other reasons for your residence here than your personal safety and health. Insanity can also lead to death." She pushed him back with enough force it made him stagger a bit before gaining his balance. "So, any thoughts you might have about possible reasons for your staying here are all about your choices, not mine. The council believed that since I was legally bound to see to your transportation and safety, you had to stay with me. I am stuck. With. You." She was leaned forward again with her rigid angry posture trying to get in his face. Then, with a gruff huff, she abandoned him in her workroom and returned to her home node probably to do another round of household chores.

She hadn't pushed for explanations regarding his condition or identity. She explained the directions of the council; keep him there and observe him during his Rite of Passage. She'd informed him that it could drive him out of his mind as it altered the body and thus one's identity so completely. Of course, there was the extreme rejection or acceptance of the changes as well which could've been included as catalysts for self-destructing.

He'd accomplished the first hurdle, he'd overcome the toxin. From memories and medical reports, he deduced the toxin was delivered in two parts; via hair styling product which was then activated by a film that remained on his mouth. He understood how he had been forced to change. All that remained was proving he was mentally stable enough to continue living his life on his terms and handle any physiological or mental developments that defy academic and scientific logic.

Since he couldn't leave at his discretion, and helping Cassie with her responsibilities was more enticing than he could indulge; he sought his work to occupy him. He manipulated figures he'd memorized from reports in plotting projects and creating solutions to existing long-standing problems he'd been putting off in order to see to other more immediate demands. When he'd return to Pater-Rio, he'd have an outline of execution and alternatives to consider based on these speculative calculations. His career may make his family and him rich, but it supported so many other people and needs in their society. He needed to keep it running.

Yet the woman kept feeding him, studying him, challenging his work ethic, and ogling him occasionally. He'd do his morning sit-ups and push-ups or twist and bends only to find her ducking out of view; regardless of where he was, outside or in. Sometimes, he'd be helping out with one chore or another to find her standing still with a dazed expression on her face. He didn't need their shared connection to know what was going on in her mind. He was, at least, discreet about his behavior.

After several weeks, his speculation work thinned and he socialized with Cassie more. He looked forward to opportunities to tease her. The stress between seeking out his hostess and alternately avoiding her combined with the need to leave had become a pressure so intense he felt ready to explode. Julius was irrelevant in helping him. By his calculations, he should be considered fine enough to be allowed to return home and work on Pater-Rio. He cycled through various ways he could abandon this planet and the non-Cassie related reasons he needed to do so. His habit to obsess about escape escalated during special moments like when she bent down to retrieve something from some low shelf or drawer within his view.

"You *are* leaving," Cassie said after cleaning a spot he believed must have been an imagined mess from the floor. She fixed her eyes to his as she stood upright and pulled her hair back to hold it high on her head. He was so distracted by her pose that he almost missed her clarification. "Well, you're leaving the hearth for a while today. You've been obsessing about your responsibilities and ditching me so well that the community believes you are firmly in possession of your sense of identity. You've created boundaries, or rather re-enforced your mental boundaries so you won't succumb to some of the hallucinations that often accompany the worst Remakings."

He was listening, but he was a little caught up in her presence. Her curves were once again disguised in her baggy, multi-pocketed, full-body covering. It was the reason why he'd thought she was a brown blob when he'd first opened his eyes during his "high." Since then, he'd corrected his initial observations, but couldn't correct his pull toward her. Even in the small amount of light streaming into the kitchen, he noted that her hair still glinted. He could've sworn glint wasn't in his vocabulary. He nodded to her as if he understood what she was saying when he had no clue.

He sat and watched her step toward him. His inner voice reminded himself of his duty to his family and employees and the consumers, and of the ramifications if a couple of other people took the helm of the company. Regardless of what he wanted, he really needed to leave.

"And we will," Cassie stepped forward leaning in face-to-face just close enough so that her curls fell around her shoulder to land on his knee.

And then he realized what she was telling him, however obliquely. "You read minds." He breathed out, slowly becoming terrified. What had he been thinking about? He'd been worried about his family and his company. And she said, "We will," to his need to contact people. He gazed at her more intently, questions swirling through his brain like a cyclone.

"It took you long enough," she snorted at him like he'd been an unobservant fool. She stepped back and turned away from him.

"I was drugged," he defended himself and subsequently started to focus on reviewing his earlier experiences with her. What could she have possibly gleaned from him while she strutted around? For whom could she be working? Had he put himself and his people in danger?

"You're focusing so hard, so clearly I can't help picking you up. But you're also blocking yourself from thinking about something. Seriously, what are you avoiding thinking about so intently that even when you don't know a telepath is in the room and you're still blocking me?" She leaned back against her counter, stretching the fabric of her clothing across her chest, with one leg bent.

"That makes no sense," he said as he massaged his eyes and avoided the distraction of her body language.

She was once again studying him. "Your mental abilities in compartmentalizing and analysis is what gave the Council optimism regarding your recovery, regardless of your foreignness to Julius."

He focused about his pet, Chiro. It was a long-necked and long-legged bird from Horto-221. It talked. It danced. And it was currently nesting in his banyan tree singing for a mate. The mate was being imported. Wait. It had arrived with that woman; he saw that mouth coming at him and his privates again. He shivered in an echo of full-body purging.

She took a long moment to blink as if she, too, was lost in a memory. "I mean, you block yourself from your own thoughts. We're going into town. There's a building we use to circumvent Julius's natural interference with communication. You'll be able to catch up on your responsibilities from there."

"Thank you," he stood, feeling as though he were regaining himself, he straightened his own burlap clothing. Absently, he wondered if they'd had other conversations where he had been responding to things she'd never said out loud.

She smiled evilly, "Don't thank me yet."

# 7

Cassie squatted on the small contraption, straddling it. It was a long, plastic, rainbow colored log. He'd seen it in the corner of her barn when they cleaned a few days past and thought it had been a kind of toy. It looked like it had two miniature saddles, the front sitting lower into the log than the one behind it. It was scaled with panels in a dizzying array of colors. "Sorry about the look, I was six and very into rainbows when my dad built it and asked me what color it should be," she apologized, seeing the look of horror on his face. She sat on the front seat pad and watched his face when she turned it on. It hovered.

"That's impossible!" he exclaimed, more offended by the violation of physics than its decoration. It wasn't enclosed. It hovered. It didn't have thrusters on the bottom to regulate height or anything for balance more than small equalizing wings. It didn't have thrusters at all, just small propulsion fans. It wasn't enclosed with an automated driver. She was moving the thing like a hummingbird by shifting the direction of fans!

"The magnetic polarity is actually strong enough to support hover trans-portation here. Propulsion is all that's needed. With a simple filtering system, we've managed to control the effect of our pollution on this planet," she frowned with guilt, "to an extent."

He could feel his blood drain from his face as he stared at where her hands pointed as she explained the device. "You're insane." She expected him to get on behind her on that six-inch wide seat. His feet were supposed to stay on that peg that was little over an inch in diameter and four inches long. He was supposed to hold onto her tiny waist in order to stay on it. She weighed about half what he did, how could she possibly counterbalance a machine that is suspended on air and anti-gravity technology?

Again, she supplied him with a toothy smile. "Absolutely," she patted the seat behind her. It didn't quite line up with her rear end, he noticed, then dragged his eyes to the padded seat where he'd straddle the thing.

"No," he felt he could've made a good impression of a rock.

"Come on," she turned it toward him and drifted around him and purred invitingly, "you'll like it."

He looked at the sky. The sun was too far away to heat this planet like this. Like didn't enter into his internal debate; the fact that the thing shouldn't exist might have if it wasn't right in front of him. But Cassie could read his thoughts. He knew showing his fear was a weakness but with her there was nothing he could hide. Though he did have some pride and he tried to use facts and logic to circumvent his aversion to this idea of riding on the hovering log with fans. It offered that tenuous hint of escape. He had many, many people depending on him. Then again, he got to touch her freely. "Stay still and go slowly."

He knew she smiled. He could feel her amusement through the threads of that webbing they shared but she gave no response to what he'd been thinking. Beneath her inviting challenge, he could also feel an unparalleled joy and anticipation associated with that machinery she flew. His anxiety tightened his hand-hold around her waist as he trusted her with their mortality. His knees gripped her hips. He had no idea how to manage his helmet-encased head, as if a helmet meant anything when their bodies were exposed to everything that could possibly happen. As she increased their speed, he debated between hunching behind her or remaining upright to see where they were going and how they were getting there. He tried both before being forced to hunker down; it soon seemed like they were speeding in hyper drive. Just when he got used to the wind, the smell, textures, and getting hit in the facemask by small living organisms with alarming crunch and crack sounds, she swerved up an arced rock and seemed to slide down it sideways without ever having touched the land. She kept rocking the damn hovering log from side to side as if bouncing off of every rock projecting four or more feet off of the ground. She'd go up one seemingly naturally formed ramp or another until they flipped in the air. "Oh. My. Stars!" he yelled when they'd flipped. Then she slowed and drove the straight and narrow for the remainder of the route, affording him a chance to relax little by little, eventually enjoying the ride.

It was a town, if an odd collection of hills unnaturally forming a circle around a shiny tower could be called a town. He watched people emerge from holes as if emerging from the public-cars' tunnels back home on Pater-Rio. Except these holes were half in the ground near domes and not into the domes, themselves. Different forms of transportation were evident; animal and machine. He eyed a traditional car without rail wheels but some other kind of substance with tread for wheels.

He let his hands span her waist, fanning his fingers out below her ribcage as much as they could. He tried to focus on the town's arrangement. There were holes in front of, but not connected to several mounds in a kind of ring. The people emerged and left with no one headed to the not-so-often used three-story tall tower in the center. Due to the winds and irregular weather patterns, of which Cassie informed him, he guessed it was best to keep most dwellings below ground.

"It has one room. We all use it. We all take turns," Cassie said when she pulled up directly to the tall, shiny, singular building. He had to center his attention on the tower and away from the loss of her body as she dismounted.

Evidently, thinking of mimicking her movement in dismounting the bike by planting one foot on the ground and lifting the other over and off proved a poor choice. His badly vibrating legs folded just after he caught his foot on the seat. He was suddenly and awkwardly seated on the ground. He reached his hands into the sands and then lifted handfuls. Large granules trickled through his fingertips.

He studied the building, hiding his embarrassment until his legs felt more like legs than folded balloons. "It looks like it's made of a kind of shiny plastic." He noticed that, like the rest of the structures on the planet, it didn't have any windows.

"The guy that built it was an historical engineer. His first career was at re-enactment bazaars; the ones where they demonstrated historically inaccurate professions. He was among the first colonists to arrive. When they realized all high technology couldn't function reliably much less indefinitely here," she turned a wheel several times in different directions on the door; then he heard the sounds of several thuds like rocks falling in a hollow pipe. She continued as they stepped through a newly opened door to proceed through a winding ascending tunnel with many more doors and air vents. "The Department of Standards disagreed with the locals' assessments and abandoned the planet designated: 'unfit to live.' He designed or reapplied some old technological innovations when frame-steel kept collapsing in and wood crumbled into shards. All navigation and stuff had to be done from orbit, an outer orbit, but they still needed the information here. The DoS couldn't acquire any reproducible data that confirmed the incongruity of the uselessness of high tech gadgetry here."

"How long ago was that?"

She shrugged as she placed her palm on the humming rectangular machine, "A couple of hundred years ago."

He waited while she went through something with which he was familiar, a bio-scanner. He watched the display for the reports and found she had several weapons on her person and that she was a healthy twenty-seven-year-old woman. "Why isn't there more in the IIN?" A question he should've asked when she explained Julius through the previous couple of weeks.

"About a quarter of the first colonists survived," she answered as he was analyzed. "They probably survived because they already had emerging non-dimensional talents and some theories on why and how to deal with them. They probably found their extra abilities magnified when someone thought bathing with the Bath Plants was a good idea. They helped as many that settled here as they could. But most of the people who came here went crazy. Some, who thought they could escape it, had to be hunted down off planet." The *because there is no escape* was left off but echoed in a brief silence.

"Yeah, you said something like that to keep me here." His mind scram-bled at her turn of phrase, "hunted down." Then, she hit him with a ball of sadness and anger through that webbing about which he occasionally forgot.

"Maybe I just want to mount your bones," she waggled her eyebrows, a non-verbal communique that he assumed transcended all cultures. His heart was still throbbing hopefully when she started pressing some buttons at an-other set of doors. She continued to speak but this time it was in an eerily quiet voice, "One guy could communicate with technology directly, accord-ing to the library we maintain. He went absolutely batty and hid it well enough no one really noticed. All he did was lay his hands on a cord and close his eyes."

"But how could he have possibly erased–"

"He merged his soul with the IIN. He became something like a thinking virus. He loaded his soul up into this, Julius's communication network and then to the IIN. He created a loop code that redirected everything about Julius to its first discoveries and assumptions about the planet. Even our landing is logged only on the local books. In the end, my ancestors realized he died to keep the people safe."

"Julius?"

"The name of the first family to die out," she answered, opening another door. It slid out in four directions. "We don't say the name of the guy. I'm not certain anyone remembers it anymore. The pages that explained why were lost in a sinkhole a few hundred years ago. His name was erased."

He grunted. His eyes took too long to adjust. The building hadn't had any windows. All he could see in this destination room was blackness. All he could feel was unmoving air. All he could hear was his heart getting louder and increasing in rhythm until she spoke.

"Lights at forty percent."

They were surrounded in a room from his grandparents' grandparents' time. The sitting area was soft and cushy, enough to lull the unsuspecting to sleep. A large viewing screen was desiccated and yet still suspended before the tables, chairs, and sofas. "This way," Cassie led him down a hall filled with doors open to small sleeping areas abandoned and sterile.

They reached a console that once had brightly colored panels coded for the users. He'd seen pictures of such panels in museums. "Uhm..." he didn't try to cover the uncertainty he felt when confronted with the panel. He just didn't know how to use it.

"Yeah, I thought so." She leaned forward, flipping on switches that created a buzz that was harsh to his ears, and turned on the screens before him. She explained most of the switches and how some view screens were new additions. Someone had to know what they were doing, adapting new technology to stuff that was so old. "Here, you go." There was no hologram equipment.

"Look, just get your work done. And then, I can dump you home." She turned but before she left the room, she used a voice he hadn't heard before. It resonated between his ears like having bass notes boom in his brain, "You don't belong here. You will not speak of Julius or anything you've found here." It made his entire body's muscles twitch for just a moment as if she were pulling on the webbing between them and at the same time pushing a ton of something, fluid, emotion, power or something through them into him; into his entire being.

# 8

Braven was pumped up with self-satisfaction when he emerged into the natural light of Julius. He eyed the beauty back-lit by the setting sun, as she was lounging too casually on that monstrosity of a transportation device. The devious look on her face was half-hidden by shadow as the sun was setting on her upturned face. She had an odd smile on her face when she met his eyes. Her burlap bag of a top was opened a bit lower than before. He could see her necklace in the shape of the statis flower dangling at the top of her cleavage. He realized she was resorting to more obvious seduction/invitation techniques than hovering nearby or the mounds of food; nevermind the bunk saying that he needed observation. With his duties seen to, he approached her with a swagger men have adopted for centuries when they were very happy to have become ensnared by the recipient of their admiration.

He splayed his hands wide on her waist and aligned his chest to her back. He breathed a compliment he couldn't remember verbatim but it was an invitation. The ride got a little shaky after that as they clarified their positions.

"I can't stay with you," he said gently, trying to assuage the guilt associated with knowing she was a woman who deserved more than a casual interlude.

"My ability doesn't promote healthy relationships. I can block for only so long," she said, her tone trying to hold a matter-of-fact tone and falling short with every moment of his hands. "I can't tolerate anyone for long," she tried to explain while her breathing became erratic. She might have said "anyone's," but his anticipation caused him to dismiss her rejection when it caused his chest to twinge for just a moment. A knoll of an oasis offered sanctuary and beckoned them as they'd not make it back to her home. He felt the light touch that was freedom knowing they could say, "good-bye" with ease.

# 9

"Nothing is manifesting," Braven declared quietly just as sleep was closing upon them. Exhausted, they lay upon their clothes, in blissful contentment and yet contemplative. He knew he sounded almost disappointed but his disappointment was that the satisfaction he achieved with her that evening didn't assuage the compulsion to be with her. She wiggled and he pulled her closer, not hearing her answer. He was caught up in contemplating the Remaking that hadn't been triggered by the planet but by a foreign substance. If anything, the planet and this woman set him to rights.

He tried to bury the complicated mass of emotions and thoughts he couldn't sift through regarding Cassie. He'd have memories. And she still shined like a light in his thoughts just as she did when he first saw her.

## 10

They were cocooned in plants the next morning. Literally, they were encased in hugging leafy greenery.

Braven ripped through them until he was out. He'd donned his coversuit at some point in the night but had tied the sleeves around his waist. Shirtless with a hand absently exploring his chest, he sought any plantlike violations. His heaving revealed that he was freaked, but, waking in a leaf and vine cocoon was a bit like being swallowed by nature. With her, though, he had no need to hide behind a wall of competence and command. "That's it. Nothing is manifesting. I have responsibilities. I have to deal with a probable attempted hostile takeover. I have to go." He turned to go. His decidedly firm footfalls stopped just short of the entrance.

He could hear Cassie slowly crawl from beneath the sheath. He knew she was still nude and used that as an excuse to give her privacy. He missed her reaction to the plants and wished he'd missed her reaction to his behavior. She chuckled at his silent but physical hysterics, "Yup."

His tension drained away. When his eyes drifted from the entrance of the node and followed the morning light until it reached the heap of decaying matter, he stepped closer to the exit. It was then he realized he couldn't meet her eyes.

From the moment they emerged from the node side-by-side, they maintained mental and audio silence until they were packed and leaving Julius.

## 11

Cassie blocked his path while boarding the ship, *Rainbow Steed*, via the cargo ramp. The sun showed on her face, while the Steed's interior lights illuminated his face. Feet firmly planted, she halted his momentum inches before colliding into her. There was no hiding.

Braven met her eyes and felt knocked to his knees again not unlike their first meeting. Except this time, he remained standing and held his ground to face her threatening expression. "This planet, however it happened, is a secret. The people here do not need to become experiments. Everyone here officially lives on ANX-321. We can't change that all electronic devices loop back to original notations of the planet. These are most of our security protocols. If inclined, you can't discuss Julius, its habitat, or its inhabitants with anyone. EVER. Remember, Braven, I brought you here in good faith to save your life."

The fact that they were engaging in real interaction, however aggressive, pleased him. He had suspicions why he was happy. Watching her chest move with her elevated breathing matched his suddenly speeding heart. He was inclined to put up his hands and say, "I got it," but curiosity claimed his diplomacy skills. He had to push, "Or what?"

"While the living virus would find and destroy electronic data, we, the people, also take our safety upon ourselves. There are several of us who can find and eliminate you anywhere. Do you understand me?" He must have looked doubtful, because she claimed, "I chauffeur some of the most prominent people on Pater-Rio because I can protect them."

He stepped closer to stare millimeters away into her eyes, "You are a pilot." His tone was dismissive of her as a threat. He stood straighter and empirically, though politely, commanded her as if she were his employee, "Now, can we please, move along? I've neglected..." And then, he was on his back, staring at the odd combination of organic and metal construction of her ship. If he tried to rewind his memory and review what happened, he'd feel the twist of wrist and arm, the pressure on his hip as she slammed into him. He'd watch the movement of the ship's walls, around his head, around his suspended feet, before he landed on his back. His hip, his knee, and arm hurt. He was laughing to himself thinking at her, *maybe I shouldn't antagonize you.*

She entered his vision, strands of hair dangled like copper coils back-lit by the ship's lights. She squatted so he could hear her, "I am a pilot and guard." She stood to tower over his prone form, "For my people, I am an Enforcer." Then, she sauntered away, providing an interesting viewpoint of her departure.

He gingerly rose to sitting, then standing. He found he wasn't particularly mad. In point of fact, he wasn't hurt. She wouldn't ever falter in her convictions, but she had cushioned his landing. Curious, he focused on the web he could still see linking them and listen to it. He heard laughter like the ones girls made in his childhood after a well-executed prank. Underneath that laughter, he felt hurt pride, hurt feminine pride.

# 12

She stayed in the pilot quarters for the trip.

He tried to visit her suite, but never gained entrance. He could've sworn she almost knocked on his, at some point, if their web was to be believed. He'd never had to apologize even when he knew he should. In this instance, he wanted to give her an apology, but lacked justification. She'd confessed that she couldn't settle in densely occupied areas for long as she couldn't block the thoughts of others indefinitely. He lived a comparatively sedentary lifestyle that could make a tool of her and possibly destroy her. Neither of them would improve the other's lives. He understood her distance and set out to emulate it.

He occupied himself during the return trip to Pater-Rio by reading the material she'd insisted upon: some copies of Julius's records regarding Re-makings. He still didn't quite understand the bits about manifesting external abilities or hyper-reactions to climates, textures, or other stimuli.

When he stood at the entrance to the cleansing cells, the first obstacle to re-entering the port of Pater-Rio's preeminent cities, he faltered. He stalled on the dock to the *Rainbow Steed*, and tried to sort through the emotions. He felt for the webbing he could no longer see. It was still strong and resilient though it didn't tell him where she was. He felt what she needed to know, that he didn't fear her seeing in his head. He needed her to know he mourned separation. And so, he walked back toward an airlock that led to the ship, which looked a bit like an iced over dust mop she'd had in her home; oblong, light green, with short dangling threads all over it. "Cassie," he called to the ship.

She came in from the shadows to his left, a storage area he hadn't noticed. "Yeah?" she seemed remote and suspicious.

Yet he could feel her telegraph her worry, her curiosity regarding the potential of their association, and the suppressed desire to touch his person. He desperately sought a reason for her to come with him, for even a short period of time, "You said medical professionals wouldn't be able to accurately detect any changes in my body. Neurologists hadn't caught up to your specialists' knowledge of the human mind."

She nodded once, "Your body may have stabilized with no ill effects of the drug, but your chemistry might fluctuate for a while after leaving Julius. Keep track of your activities; both actually taken and those you considered but discarded. Also observe your environment. You might need to sort through your thoughts and decisions versus someone standing next to you, even plants. You've watched the graph of the history of Julius, the advice passed through generations." He smiled to himself as she shifted under his studious gaze. She glanced at the cleansing chamber that lead to the busy corridors as if it were an escape.

"I have to check to see if I have clients," she said. Her statement confirmed his suspicions because he knew she could check on that from her ship's console. His wants and what he suspected she wanted clarified to him when she asked, "How about we walk and talk?"

# 13

Upon officially entering the port corridors, they saw a reflection of their images emerging in real time on the newscycler, the flashing narrow billboard of news that traveled the tops of corridors and entryways all through the port. His face emerged alongside hers as if they were a pair of the Most Wanted. They were wanted in connection to a kidnapping reported by his family and investors. He needed to get rid of the notification circling around their heads on the newscycler before they went any further and were rounded up by the MSP, the Multinational Security Personnel. He approached a camera and stated very clearly, "I will attest that Cassie Wiche and I, Braven Clair, have become companions since that footage was recorded." He read the tagline on the image indicating date and location of the footage of Cassie catching his collapsing form that had been airing. "Research the recordings from earlier in the hour of our departure. You'll see I was very ill. As I paid for premier treatment, she was bound to see to my welfare and whim. Cease all investigation at this moment in time. Record timestamp. Forward statement to all branches of the Multinational Security Personnel."

Braven pulled Cassie forward and brushed a kiss along her cheek. He pulled information from that webbing to gauge how to execute his plan. The shock of his declaration had stunned her while his kiss on her cheek scattered her mental skills. He suppressed his pride in her response to him before he leaned into her, "I apologize for this."

It was then he was warned by the look in her eyes and the hand on the back of his head that she decided that she needed to take control. When he began to discretely nuzzle her cheek with his to hide conversation, she turned her face. She met his lips with her demanding and possessive kiss. Angling just so, she managed to wring a gutturally pleased sound from him as their kiss morphed into one that threatened to buckle both of their knees. Applause broke them apart.

He ignored the replay of their kiss on the newscycler. Instead, he rested his forehead to hers, breathing heavily as he spoke, "They'll be watching to assure themselves that I am not under duress." He draped an arm around her shoulders and turned them to walk further into port. For the benefit of the camera, he said, "You'll have to stay with me for a while to show we're partners." He whispered to her and added an out clause for her, "For now. Unless you want to be inspected every time you dock?" He hoped she understood that it was a warning and not a threat.

"Yeah, I can do that," she remarked with her heart speeding up and resolution on her face.

"Just use your web thing to tell me if they do anything that might threaten you. I'll try to help you live as quietly as possible when we're together here." He had a new small headache. He didn't think it had anything to do with the huge mass of anxiety and hope that just spiraled through the web from Cassie colliding with his own. It could be the strengthening of the web bing between them, or it might be the "gift" from the toxic revamp to his body. Or something else could be afoot.

"What web?" Alarm and suspicion mixed in her quiet voice.

*Oooops,* he thought at her. He smiled at her surprised eyes. *There's been something I've been meaning to ask about.*

# OTHERKIN

## BY STEVEN INMAN

### 1

I thought I knew a lot about Elena but in the end it was really very little. We were both housekeepers at the Manhattan, Kansas Holiday Inn: I'd been there for two years and Elena a week or so. I hadn't really talked with Elena, hadn't even noticed her until one Tuesday in April. It had been raining for three days, and everyone was in a good mood because of the rare precipitation, everyone except the Housekeeping Manager. She handed me a clipboard with my list of rooms for the day, and there were some on a floor I don't normally do. "Elena called out, no surprise," she told me. "If she wasn't so new I'd fire her."

"Elena?" I asked.

The manager tapped my clipboard. "Elena's usually on the sixth floor. She likes the top, for some reason."

I rode up in the elevator with Ulyana the Russian. When she saw me, Ulyana said, "Hi Marcie." And then nodded knowingly. "Elena. She always calls... when it rains. Must make her sick, you know, no rain anymore."

"You mean no rain for four months and then a downpour," I corrected. I tried to remember this new girl Elena – I think at that point I'd seen her a few times. "She doesn't look too strong," I commented.

Ulyana nodded. "Yeah, you need to be strong. Carts are heavy."

I nodded my head. "No kidding. Well, maybe you're right, maybe Elena caught a flu or something."

"Yes." Ulyana waved a hand. "She is always that way. Sick."

The other sixth floor housekeeper, Deb, was loading her cart in the closet, stuffing too many sheets onto the sides. She nodded when she saw me, knowing who'd called out. "Her eyes, you seen them?" Deb said. "Always with shadows under them." She stuffed even more sheets onto the cart. "Elena's nice, willing to work, but she never seems fully charged."

"Never fully charged" nailed it for me, and I didn't think much of someone who came in half-charged. And at lunch Deb told me how Elena was being a shy one... quiet. Loner. Elena will be out as long as it's raining.

The rain stopped the next afternoon, and Elena came in the day after that... and that's when I first really wondered about her. Elena came back, and she did not look as if she had *ever* been sick. I'd been in enough jobs to know the slackers – *skaters* we called them – and how they'd claim sickness but come back looking normal.

Elena didn't come back looking normal. She returned looking better than normal: she *shone*, as if something had given her some new inner glow.

## 2

We were on separate floors and everyone took their breaks at different times so there wouldn't be much chance of us meeting. But for some reason –

maybe that shine in her – I tried to catch sight of Elena outside during her breaks. Most of us went to the smoke shack even if we didn't smoke, but Elena sat off to one side. Sometimes someone sat with her, sometimes not. She didn't seem to mind either way, and I eventually timed my breaks to hers and managed to sit beside her. "Smoke doesn't blow over here," I pointed out.

Elena smiled at me, warm but not too open. "No," she answered. "No, it doesn't." This was a week or more after the rain, and I noticed that she was looking more like her normal self: tired. We talked about the usual stuff, the hotel guests and the way they left their rooms, the lack of pay and the hard times.

She pulled her top closer on her shoulders, tightened her arms in, as if chilled. She noticed my noticing and shivered. "Cold for April," she said to me, and her voice was low: pleasant, but weak. You had to focus to listen to her, but once you heard her you kept listening. "But I get cold easy when it's so dry."

"We had a wood stove when I was a kid," I told her. "My father put a big pot of water on it, said that humidity makes the air feel warmer."

She nodded, and I asked where she was from, if she'd grown up in Kansas. "Mostly." She answered. "We..." there was a little hesitation, "...we didn't have a wood stove. I used to warm up in a hot shower."

"My favorite way too," I said, and over at the smoke shack Karla, who'd been trying to adjust her uniform, slipped off the curb, and we laughed at that. "Makes the day go faster," I said. "Laughing at something."

We met like this a few times a week, and at one point I realized that not only was this seat a distance away from the smoke shack, it was the one close by the outdoor pool. This swimming pool was new; instead of chlorine and chemicals like the indoor pool this outside one had a saline system. It was supposed to stay clean without the chemicals. There was a pile of rocks at one end, and the water came out the top, tumbled down like a waterfall, splashing. I liked the sound, and I think Elena did too. Sometimes I would find her sitting there, arms tight against her chest, eyes closed.

And on we cleaned, day after day, room after room. A few weeks later, Mid-May, there was a series of bad storms, with a lot of steady rain. Business slumped off for a few weeks, and we were all down to four days. There really wasn't much to do or catch up on, and we rarely hung out with each other.

That Friday I ran into her downtown. We said hello, she said she was walking home, and since I was in the general direction we went together, making idle talk.

Then I noticed that every so often she would sort of stray to one side or another: a few times she actually took a bunch of steps away from me. I snickered at her, asked if she'd been drinking, but she just made her small careful smile.

I watched her, and saw what it was: she was touching water. All the rain had left puddles and pools, small trickles and larger runoffs from buildings. Whenever one came near Elena would absently move toward it and sift her feet – in open sandals – through the puddles, or slowly pass a hand beneath rainwater falling from a spout. Her hands, her arms were glistening with water, as if it did not want to dry off. I guess I laughed again, and I know I said, "You like water, don't you?"

Elena paused, caught off-guard and looked at her arm, her hand. Then she looked up at me, and for a moment I really couldn't tell what she would do. I knew I'd said something that held more meaning for her, something that could really... hurt, or shock, I guess. I remember that look from my mom when I was a kid and said something I thought funny, like, "Oh my aching ass." Mom would get that look, I couldn't tell if she was going to laugh or whack my head. You can guess which I usually got.

With Elena, though, it was like that but without the slap heading my way. She looked at her arms, her hands, and lifted her eyes to mine. "Marcie..." she said, as if she'd just met me. "I guess I do."


# 3

We met more after that. Breaks, lunch, after work walks home. A lot of times we didn't talk, which was fine for us both. Housekeeping is back-breaking work, bending over beds, scrubbing bathroom floors and shower walls, pushing heavy carts through carpeted halls, and sometimes a knowing glance or single word was enough to make a point.

On one Saturday I mentioned my brother's birthday approaching, and the usual cookout with his family. Elena listened, her head cocked toward me, her footsteps slow. Her steps were always slower than me because her legs were so long.

Matter of fact, her whole body was long and tall. She always seemed thin, but smooth as well. I figured an artist could sketch her with a few mildly curved lines.

She asked about my family, I asked about hers, if there were any in the town. She sort of smiled, sadly, and said no. "They're gone."

"Gone?" I asked. "I'm sorry... do you mean they've all died?"

She looked at me again, then away, toward the distance. "I guess so. I was brought up over on Newcomb Street."

"Newcomb?" I asked.

She made a vague point with her head, long black hair swinging. "Not far from here," she said,but her eyes seemed to go really distant. "Foster parents. I was an orphan. My parents died young, when I was four."

"Sorry to hear that." There's that awkward hesitation, when you don't know if it's better to ask more or keep shut. Being me, I asked. "Any brothers or sisters?"

Elena shook her head. "No." Her long slow steps stayed beside me. She pursed her lips and glanced toward me. "Don't worry about me... I grew up this way. I'm not too sociable anyway."

"Hmm," I sort of agreed.

Elena was silent for a bit, thinking, it seemed, about something. We crossed Pace Avenue and Wilkes, and up ahead I had to turn left. As we approached the intersection Elena laid a hand on my arm. "Can you walk a bit, to my place?" There was that faint sort of smile. "I want to show you something."

An invitation like that is always double-edged, and you know that whatever your choice is you are going to go somewhere different. "Sure," I said. After all, she'd been good to me.

Her place was small but nice, the second floor of an old small house.

Kitchen, living-dining, bedroom and bathroom. Not much closet space but she didn't seem to have a lot. Two of those water fountain things that make a nice rippling sound. An aquarium. And strange... a water cooler, the kind you see in offices. Elena dropped her bag on a couch and went into her bedroom. "You don't like the city water?" I asked.

She shrugged as she came back out. "I can drink it." A small motion with her head pointed to the faucet. "But no, I don't like it. They make the city water safe but... it's dead."

"That's the truth." I agreed. "You ever use the indoor pool at work? We can, you know, as long as it's your off day and it's not busy."

Her face darkened a bit. "I don't like it. Chlorine, chemicals," she brightened a little and peered at me, then whispered, secretly, "I use the outside pool."

I made a fake gasp. "We're not supposed to."

Another look, meaning *I know.*

"Well, I'm not talking," I promised. We smiled together, and hers, for once, looked like it had a bit of happiness in it. There was a pause and then she handed me a picture, a small one, framed. I took it, and then found a seat and dropped into it to examine the image.

Old and in black and white, cracked, drying up: but the image was simple and unearthly. If you saw a picture of a woman, in a white gown, floating in water with her eyes closed, you would think she's dead, a dead body. But this woman was what my dad would call sublime, and it was clear that she was very much alive and in her element. You couldn't even see the water really; just guess it was there because the woman floated in it, a pale form in deep blackness. I handed it back to Elena, finally, not sure what to say. "She's beautiful. It's a... a great picture."

"My mother," Elena said. "That's what the state worker gave me, this, some clothes, and a birth certificate."

"Your mother?" I stood and went beside Elena to look over the picture again. "It's an impressive picture. It looks professional. Was she in a movie?"

Elena shrugged, and then suddenly began fumbling with the frame. "I know her name, of course. It's on the birth certificate. Dina McLayne." Elena had opened the frame and removed the picture; she handed it to me, pointing with her long finger. On the back was written: Atargartis at Weeki Wachee 1960.

"Atargartis at Weeki Wachee?" I asked. "What does that mean?"

Elena took the picture back and replaced it in the frame. "That... it's, well, I'm not sure. I looked these things up. Atargartis is the mother of all mermaids. Weeki Wachee is a place in Florida. It's a resort, and they put on a mermaid show. The swimmers breathe through tubes, swim around. I don't know. 1960 is probably when it was taken."

" 'Mother of all mermaids...' " I repeated. "So I guess that's why you like water." I caught a faint, uneasy look passing over Elena's face, but she said nothing. I went on: "So it is your mom?"

Elena nodded. "The social worker said it was. It was with her..." She took a breath before going on: "...She drowned, up in Tuttle Creek. This was in her purse on the beach. This, a few dollars, some makeup."

"Weird," I said. "It seems she swims as a job, someone calls her the mother of mermaids, and she *drowns*. I'm sorry, I don't mean to sound cold. It's just... tragic."

Elena made a face: *it is what it is*, and I really didn't know what to say after that, other than I had to get home. I thanked her though, and told her the picture really was beautiful, and I appreciated seeing it. Elena nodded, opened the door, but like in a TV show I paused at the door, almost smiling. "I can see some of her in you. Especially the water part."

"Especially the water," Elena laughed.

I laughed too, and touched her arm. "Hey, and thanks for showing me."


## 4

But on Tuesday, back at work, Elena told me not to think she was crazy. "I am not a mermaid," she half-joked. "No tail. I can't breathe water." She drank some from a bottle. "Once in a while I choke while drinking. And I was born in a hospital, with doctors watching."

"Sure," I replied. "But if a great flood ever comes I am staying with you."

We laughed.

I do that, laugh things off. But through that day I thought of a girl, grow-ing up alone, with that picture of her mother in the water and the nickname Atargartis. How much that girl would want a mother, and idolize that picture. Staying out in the rain, splashing through puddles, stealing swims in the salt water pool at night: imagining herself to be that special orphan, like every or-phan's dream.

One day I asked Elena why she was in Manhattan, why didn't she move to the coast, near the ocean. She gave me the look that everyone in this type of work knows: *move? On this pay?*

"Any idea why your mother was here? No mention of her parents being here?"

Elena shrugged, looking tired, and I realized she must have gone through this a lot. *Who were my parents, my family? What was their history?* She did tell me a few bits and pieces, of stories that her mother had been out of work, had been abandoned by her husband, and had sought some escape from something here, in Kansas. Maybe a final escape in Tuttle Creek.

We talked for a while; there isn't much else to do on breaks or on days off. The rain had pretty much left us until the fall and while the heat wasn't excessive, it was dry. Not just dry, but dust-in-your-eyes dry. So we just sat and talked. And not always about her: Elena wanted to know of my life, my family, so I told her all I knew. Things had been bothering me the way family stuff does, and sometimes after telling it all to someone it doesn't seem so bad.

It seems funny, that all this time – it was the middle of June now – I'd been thinking of this water and mermaid stuff but I'd never actually seen her in water. It happened that as we talked about family one day, I told her I was going to Tuttle Creek for a picnic with my brother and his wife and kids. "Come with us," I said. "At the least we can swim, get out of this dry heat, soak up some water."

It only took a little convincing, and we did have a good time. My brother's wife isn't shy but she is quiet, sort of serene, and they got along nicely. We ate and played, but I could tell Elena was distracted, working ever-so-slightly at being nice. Ten minutes after arriving we were ready for the water, and Elena was wise enough to stay out of the way and let the kids barrel in. And yes, I side-ways watched as she pushed off her clothes: she had a one-piece suit underneath, and again, under that suit I could see a nice form, something that could be athletic if it wasn't way too weak and pale.

My nephews were shouting and splashing, so my brother ran, dove, tucked in his legs and made a huge splash. Anna and I walked in with grace of course, sort of dropping down into the water.

Elena came last, walking in slowly, eyes glistening as the water crept up her legs. Then she sort of shifted and leapt, her body arcing out and almost melting into the water with hardly a splash. And she pretty much spent the day there, swimming circles around us.

# 5

And then my mouth got me into trouble. We were working together the day after that Tuttle Creek visit, cleaning one of the suites, after a bachelor party. We'd sat at the table, resting, when I mentioned that picture of her Mom again, how beautiful it was. And I asked Elena what it had been like to grow up and see only that one image of her mother.

Elena's mouth tightened, and eyes grew distant. "I..." her voice was always soft, and hesitant. "It gave me something. Kept me going."

"I guess," I said. "I imagine it's good to have just that one image, I guess. I got to see the good and bad of my parents, knew them *too* well at times." I cleared my throat, trying to clear my thoughts. "I think that's why you love water so much, I guess."

Elena looked at me. But her eyes held no caution, no fear. "What do you think?" she asked me, and her question was genuine, interested.

So I finished: "I think you sort of steer yourself into a water-lover, mermaid idea because you only see that image of your mother. You try to follow that." Elena watched me another moment before turning away, and I spent the rest of our time in that room trying to soften the idea, to backpedal. To say that it was a *good* thing, to model yourself after your mother.

Elena said little until we left the room. Then, as we closed the door and before she headed back to six and me to the rest of four, she looked at me and said: "It's... a craving. No... more of a hunger, like a need. I need to be in water." She looked down and walked to the elevators.

# 6

We worked together a bit, off and on over the next month but business picked up a bit and my life did as well, so we didn't see too much of each other. Not that we were unfriendly or mean, just that my stupid mouth and what I said cooled things for a bit, which was probably good, things were a touch flaky.

A new guy had started at the Inn, working the eleven-to-seven audit shift. Somehow he hooked up with Elena and I was a little pleased: he seemed like what you'd call a nerd. I figured this was a good match.

I teased her a bit, the way people do: "So, you got yourself a boyfriend..." I was afraid she would get angry, or embarrassed, but the look she gave me made me feel dumb all over again. I realized that she'd probably had boyfriends before, and that I was assuming her to be some naive kid.

"I like him," Elena was saying to me. "He is a decent guy." Her eyes narrowed as she thought. She bowed her head, shyly. "He saw me in the pool one night. That's how we met, he came over and wasn't mad or anything. Just curious."

"I hope you were wearing a suit." I joked, and Elena's look made me wonder if she sometimes didn't.

"It's good," she went on. "It helps me, to be around other people. I know I'm a recluse," she finished her water and made a face, her lips tightening. "Ever since you said that about me wanting to follow my mother."

"Yeah, I'm sorry about that."

"No..." she shook her head but didn't pat my hand: somehow she seemed both faded *and* strong. "No, it was good. Has me thinking. I just have this... draw, to be in water. To feel it. I..." she laughed. "When I was a kid I did think at times I was a mermaid, a Nereid or undine or something. But I mean, what you said means a lot."

"Does he help? Do you talk with him about this?"

She nodded. "He tries to understand. He said I should..." she sighed. "Said I should go to Topeka with him. There's a big thing there, some people meeting, and they play around."

Play around? I thought that sounded sketchy, but Elena went on: "He said it is about costumes, people are pretty serious about it. And it seems safe."

I'd heard of it, seen some pictures. Adults dressed up like comic figures, or movie characters. "Cosplay," it's called, and you can't get much geekier than that, and it hardly seemed like anything Elena would be around. But maybe it would be good for her. Get her out of her shell.

Later, though, the idea bothered me. It seemed undignified for her. There would be women dressed like some fish-mermaid-creatures, and there would be Elena, swimming in the hotel pool at night, floating between light and dark, like her Mom.

# 7

Elena was becoming more detached. She still talked with me, but there was a different focus in her. Like her eyes were on something else, off to one side.

Whatever happened with the cosplay stuff I don't know. I tried to find out. I would get in to work a little early, manage to be around the audit guy – Ned. Said I was Elena's friend, and eventually I managed to get him to show me some pictures of the convention. Like I thought, there were people dressed up. It did look fun, everyone had genuine smiles and there seemed to be a lot of good will and cheer. But Elena wasn't in any of the pictures, and when I pressed I found that they weren't together anymore. "She's nice," Ned told me. "I like her. But I think I was a little too geeky for her." He shrugged.

"Was it the convention?" I asked.

He shrugged again. "She didn't dress up," he promised. "She was like she usually is – kind of apart, you know? Not snobby, just... separate." He rubbed his chin, and then ran a hand through his hair. "She did appreciate it, she met this other lady there, and they talked." Ned blinked, as if he'd let out too much.

"She likes ladies?" I asked, not one to be shy.

But Ned shook his head at that. "No, it wasn't that. Though..." he wrinkled his face in thought. "That never came across my mind, because she seems so... apart from anything people are doing..." I was about to push again when Ned came back to reality. "No, this lady was there but didn't have anything on the agenda. Sort of a quiet sideline thing."

"A sideline thing?" I pushed. That sounded doubtful.

"Otherkin," Ned actually blushed. "She was telling Elena about Otherkin."

## 8

This was an education for me. Ned didn't seem eager to explain anything and I was not going to ask Elena, so I went to the library. What I found, for what it was worth, was... interesting. Made me think a long time. Otherkin are those people who believe they are something else trapped in a human body. Dragons, elves, wizards, warriors or beings of ethereal light.

Or mermaids.

I didn't know whether to worry or not. I mean, thinking you're a dragon in a human body? I wasn't going to argue with anyone over what they believe but how normal is that?

I sat at home at night and thought of these things. It was like evidence was building, but for what? Elena was not guilty of anything, had every right to all this, to think she was a mermaid if she wanted. At work, when we talked, she was maybe a little more withdrawn, as if she was thinking of all these things but was afraid to confide in anyone. I finally told her what I'd learned, but she didn't seem too surprised. Grateful, appreciative, but not surprised. "Thank you for doing that," she told me, and she put her hand on mine. "For looking that up. For being interested." I don't know if that changed anything. Her work at the hotel was still good, and she was not going crazy, so I should have let it go.

But some part of me felt a shift in Elena, and somehow it was affecting me. I could not look away.

# 9

"Are you growing a tail under those clothes?" I asked her one day. We were outside, cleaning the pool patio after a party. It was a mess. I was picking up cups and bottles; Elena was emptying and cleaning coolers. I felt bad for her and the mess. I could see her out of the corner of my eye, her hands going in and out of coolers, probably fishing out cigarette butts.

She straightened and made her pale, soft laugh. "No, I promise," she brushed her hair back and looked at the sky. "I wouldn't mind it, sometimes, but it'd be hard to get around on land."

We chatted for a bit as we cleaned. She didn't seem to be doing any better with the coolers, though; she seemed distracted and slow. I worked to finish the tables so I could help her. As I cleaned my last table I asked over my shoulder about people and their past lives, about being someone else. "I mean..." I worked to get it out right, "...like you, having this inner thing so strong that it is... well, *you*, inside a different body. Like those transgender sorts."

Elena glanced at me. "Like the Otherkin," she replied, sounding a bit suspicious of me, of my thoughts on the matter.

I waited, and Elena sat on a patio chair, her hand playing with the ice in a cooler. I sat beside her; we were due for a break anyway. She rattled some cubes and went on. "I like the group. They're nice, and they seem real. Whether you believe them or not you have to admit that they really...," she shifted and met my eyes, keeping her hand in the cooler. "Marcie. This is what I thought: a person might believe that they are a dragon-spirit in a human body, but a doctor who examines them would find only a human body. But if you could look at their *mind*, you might see that they really believe they are a dragon. So are they?"

"I think some are just confused young people," I had to be honest. "They don't fit in so they make up something like that, and it makes them feel spe-cial."

Elena nodded. "Yes, there are those," her tone made it clear she'd dealt with them, and dismissed them. "But at what point does what they believe become real?"

I shook my head. "So you think that if someone believes hard enough – that they're a dragon – then they'll grow wings?"

"No." Elena looked down, mixed between embarrassment and confusion. And something else. "No," she repeated. "I mean, they say that their body is human but their soul is one of a dragon. Who can argue with that, who can look at their soul and say it is or isn't?"

That sounded dangerous to me, this idea that if you believe in something hard enough it can become real. It's how cults get started, how people get crazy or hurt, mentally, maybe physically.

"That can be dangerous," I finally said. "Because if you believe hard enough that you are a dragon trapped in a human body, then you start not lik-ing your body. Hating it." I stood and shook my head, again. "That can't be healthy."

Elena saw my thoughts on my face, because she started shaking her head as she rattled more ice cubes. "It's just that... there are people with all sorts of... unusual beliefs," she said. "But I agree. You can't just wish something and it's true. If anything, it must be more like aspiring to be an athlete. You want it, you feel this desire consume you and envelope you. You only feel joy when you are performing. But that desire alone is not enough. You must train, with skill and attention."

I couldn't say much to that, only a mutter of agreement; and break time was over anyway, by the looks of the manager glaring at us out the window. I stood, but Elena kept her hand in the ice a moment longer. I looked down, thinking she'd had that hand in there for fifteen or twenty minutes now, it must be all pruny and pale. But the hand was bright, about as healthy looking as could be, and almost all the ice was gone, melted to water. As I watched she lifted her hand, holding a couple of cubes. In an instant the cubes were gone, the water remaining for a second too long, clinging to her skin.

# 10

She was intriguing. I say that because at some point in this story people wonder why we were even friends. I mean, I'm outspoken, fun-loving but serious about work and moving up, serious about what needs to be serious and ready to enjoy life in everything else. Elena, she wasn't depressed or reclusive, but like Ned told me, she was apart. There was a slow sadness in her. Her body didn't seem healthy; she was thin and pale. Weak, in spite of this sense of distant lost strength. She lit up at anything to do with water, and there seemed to be a deep peace in her... but the sadness was slowly growing. Slowly taking over like a steady tide.

So yeah, we stayed friends. For my part I think Elena saw something in me, but I have no idea what. I tried to get to know more of these Otherkin, and Elena tried to describe what it was like. One day she went on about another group that was doing Fursonas – dressing as animals – and their Yiffs – meaning an aggressive hello or come-on. I knew it was mean but I couldn't help but giggle, and Elena ended up laughing as well. Not that I should laugh at anyone, considering some of the things I do, which I will not mention.

Another time we were looking over some pictures of a super-hero movie coming out. The actors were wearing costumes, of course. "I have to be honest," I said. "When a person wears a costume, it's to make him feel better, have fun. At Halloween, or a party, you hide behind it, so you can whoop it up. But to wear one around just, in..."

"Daytime?" she suggested, with a smile.

I slapped her lightly. "Yeah, daytime. A costume then is covering up something. Like low self worth. I think that's why you didn't get into that cosplay thing with Ned."

"Maybe," she sort of agreed. "Maybe they are having a good time, just not one I want. But there's the other side of it too." I waited, and Elena finished; "Maybe it's not just about putting a costume on, but about taking one off."

"Yeah," I said, in my way I do when I'm not thinking it through, "taking it off." Elena just gave me her careful, low smile, like she was waiting for it to sink in.

A few days later it did. Take off the *human* costume. "Neat idea." I muttered to myself in my tiny kitchen. "Good movie stuff." And I had to wonder: how far did they think they could take it? I mean, what are they going to do, skin someone and then say *whoops, no dragon wings? No mermaid tail?*

# 11

"Don't worry," Elena promised me on Friday. It was a day off for us both but it was also payday and we both had rent due. We walked back along Poytnz Ave, toward the credit union. "There are plenty of people who are just..." she paused, and then went on: "...most people believe in some after-life. That you die, and then you are something else. Spirit, or a new body, something."

"A caterpillar," she said a minute later. "When it starts to change into a butterfly, everything about it that's caterpillar becomes old. Almost alien. It knows there is something else in its body, coming out."

I laughed. "Every time I hear you talk about these Otherkin I get a different picture of them. I think I want to meet them; they're sounding more and more interesting."

"Really?" Elena kept walking, but I could hear the pause, the catch in her voice. Then she looked at me, her lips tight, eyes narrowed. "I really don't meet with them anymore."

I did stop then. "Why? Not something I said, is it?"

She shook her head quickly. "No, no, Marcie. You help me. You help clear my head."

She seemed unsure, so I was thinking of what to say to prompt her, when it occurred to me. "You've moved on. You met some other group. Like the cosplay didn't cut it, and now the Otherkin."

And she gave me one of her rare laughs. I don't want to sound like I prefer women, not that there's anything wrong with it, I'm as open-minded as the next lady... but anyway, I loved her laugh. It was not delicate, but not loud either, just pleasant. Anyway, she told me. "I met another man. His name is Ry. His parents named him Ryobi."

"Ry," I repeated. "I like that one. Better than being named after a power tool."

"Yes. His parents are not... exactly the same as he is," Elena replied. "He uses Ry, but he spells it R-Y-E."

"Rye," I repeated yet again. "Like the bread."

"Or the grain. It's sort of a half-joke," Elena looked up at me, and this time she didn't seem shy or hesitant, but excited. Almost eager. "I want you to meet him."

## 12

I invited the two of them to my place for dinner, thinking it would be as good a place as any to eat. When I made the invitation, Elena tightened her lips, looked away for a second, and I could see the *no* coming. "Whatever you want is fine with me," I quickly added. "I don't want to scare him. There's a big field behind the house, and I just thought we'd sit outside and watch the sun go down over the grass."

Elena lit up when I told her that, she agreed, and we set a date. I whipped up a lasagna and salad and bread, something I hadn't done in a long time.

When they showed up at my door I had a brain cramp, wondering what to call the guy. But Elena introduced him as Rye, so I went with that. He was nice, thin but wiry-strong, open sort of eyes and face, long-ish hair but neat. "I'm Rye during the day," he said as he walked in. "But I think I might use my middle name – Mike – at work. Rye is starting to get on my nerves, and Ryobi got on my nerves a long time ago."

We had fun. He was nice, open and honest. We laughed a lot during the meal, made plenty of jokes, talked about work and life in general. I didn't see any sappy puppy-love between them, for which I was glad, and there wasn't any serious thing either. At least, not at that point. But he clearly respected her, and there was some start of affection, showing a little more than usual help, clearing her plate, small touches.

Of course I was waiting for the "thing," the reason Elena had moved on from the other stuff to this guy. Was he a merman, or something else?

The back of the house faced the west, and the bright setting sun had made the deck too uncomfortable for dinner. We all cleaned up in my small kitchen, Elena washing and Rye drying, and me putting stuff away. I asked him about his childhood, where he grew up.

"Kansas," he smiled. "The left side of the state, near Colorado."

"The big plains," I replied. "Not much out that way."

And he smiled again, handing me a plate. "No, that was lucky for me." Elena's hands stopped, and she flashed him a small look. Rye touched her lightly on the small of her back, and lifted another plate to dry. "The town I grew up in was small. Hugoton, down near the Cimarron Grasslands. My mother was a clerk; now she runs a small bank in town. My father is a farm mechanic."

"They're still there?" I asked. "Do you get back much?"

He shrugged. "I need to eat, I need a job, and there's not much there. But it's my home, so yes, maybe twice a month."

I nodded, took his towel since we'd finished. "I know the feeling. Some people love to move and go all over but I want to stay right in the same kind of place I grew up in." He nodded, agreeing, and I went on: "And it's good that you get along with your parents."

He laughed. "Not always, but usually." We were all just standing in the kitchen, a little awkwardly I thought, with it being so small. Then Rye glanced at Elena, then me. "Elena's talked with you about her life..."

I began to nod but Elena took hold of his elbow. "We should walk," she said, in her soft, direct voice. "The sun's down and it's nice out now."

So I guess this was the first time I began to understand them. I thought we'd go out the front, walk along the streets for a bit, see the people and the sights. But Elena tilted her head toward the back door. "In the fields," she said. "It's nice right now."

I really hadn't spent much time in the... well, in nature, I guess, since I was a kid. Bugs, dirt, and yes there are some beautiful places in the world but the middle of Kansas is pretty bleh. So I looked at her and shrugged. "In the fields, sure."

Out we went, across the lawn and into the grass. It was a large area of field, maybe a few hundred acres, and there were a few distant buildings on the far side. Not quite open plains but near enough. The farmer who ran it had run feed corn but let it go these last two years, so now it was a nice hay-mix: timothy and clover and a dozen other plants I didn't know. I wasn't even sure I had the timothy and clover right. But whether you know the names or not, it's peaceful and... apart from the rush of everything. You feel the plants move along your skin, hear the thin soft rustle and notice the variety of color in what you thought was just greens and browns, and pretty soon you are removed from the everyday world.

As we passed into the chest-high grass I made a comment to Rye: "You must know all these, growing up in the country."

He made a slow sort of nod. "More or less." He said it like he knew but didn't really worry about proper names. And as he walked into the field I noticed his arms hung out a bit, hands open to the plants as they brushed him. Just like Elena, every time she passed a bit of clear water.

We were out there a while and said very little. Matter of fact, I can't even say now what it might have been that we said. All I remember is that Rye seemed to wake up, somehow. I mean, when we had been eating I thought he was what they call charismatic. Something about him that seemed very centered and alive. But walking in the grass behind him, I felt more at peace and at home than I ever had in nature, and it was because he was there and I was watching him just being himself.

And Elena, walking beside him, looked as pale and tired as ever, but she smiled as she watched Rye, knowing what it meant to her own life.

# 13

It was tragic, in the end. Like Romeo and Juliet, but without the blood and death. Rye lived for the Plains, he was a creature of open sky and expansive lands, and he could not live anywhere else. Elena loved the open air, but needed water between her toes. They knew it couldn't last, but were living in the moment.

From what I could gather, from what Elena told me and what I saw in her face, it seemed that they dated for a while. Went out together, talked a lot. A few times when we visited or I saw him pick her up after work, Rye looked – no matter what the mood – at peace with the world.

Elena, though, continued to fade, her face growing paler, eyes darker. We hadn't had rain in months, and streams were drying up. Water was on tight controls again, no washing cars, water lawns once a week, and so on. Everyone was appreciating moisture, and Elena wasn't the only one running her hands under faucets, feeling for drips, or walking dry stream beds, rolling over rocks for tiny puddles.

# 14

We slid into August, then September, and on October 10th Elena gave her notice. I was torn. On one hand I thought it was good – *great* – that she dumped this stupid hotel and followed her own path. But on the other hand I was afraid for what that path would be: wandering around with people who think they're mermaids, or dragons. Even if she grew a tail she would still need to eat; she couldn't just up and quit. *Have some common sense*, I wanted to tell her. *Be realistic*.

But I said nothing, and two weeks later we had the pizza lunch and a card with forty-two names crammed in it, and it was goodbye. I waited a few more days before walking over to her apartment. She was still there, and nothing was packed – though it would not have taken much to pack the few things she owned.

"I found a job," she said. "Online, on the company website." She was talking fast, as if trying to calm me; maybe she expected me to be angry with her.

"That's good!" I told her. "I love to see someone move up. I would, if I didn't like this city so much."

Elena smiled at me, pulling her hair back. I patted her arm and asked where she was headed.

She seemed unsure, and her expression got dark, almost sadder. "Mon-tana," she finally answered, in a small voice. "There's a small hotel there. The

Big Sky Inn. And the same job: housekeeping."

"Wow," I said, unsure. "Why Montana?"

She shrugged. Then sat down, shrugged again, stood, went to the bar stool and sat again. "You know I've been through things this last year," she wasn't looking at me as she gathered her thoughts. "I have been trying to find out... not so much where I belong, but where I am now. What I am."

My mouth opened but Elena smiled and looked up, held up her hand. "I'm human, I know. That's not what I meant. You know there's more to it," she looked down again, and I could see she was trying to figure out what to tell me. Finally it was just: "I need time alone, away from everything I know. To sort things out."

"I can understand that," I replied. "And I agree with that. I think it's great, what you're doing."

"Thank you." She carefully stood, bracing herself on the counter, and touched my arm with her cool hand. We talked a while longer, about all sorts of stuff but mainly work and weather, men and the world in general. I brought up Montana a few more times, tried to hear more of her thoughts, what she planned – what she expected would happen there – but she didn't say much.

Before I left Elena asked me to take her fish. She'd moved them into a small container for carrying – she said she'd bring me the tank and pumps later – and she went into the bathroom to get them. While I waited I looked over some papers on her table. Bills, of course, change of address cards, and a map of central Montana, with her new town circled in blue.

And running from that town was a line, drawn in red, leading to a nearby lake.

# 15

Life gets busy. Elena brought the tank and pumps over and helped me set up her fish. I wanted to ask about the lake but something held me back.

And life stayed busy, so I didn't get back to Elena's apartment until ten days later. She was gone by then, of course. Someone else had already moved in, a middle-aged guy, nice, said he wasn't the smartest but could fix anything and if I needed car repairs to just stop in. He seemed honest and safe enough, and I said I just might, if I ever get a car.

A thousand thoughts ran through my head for months. Why Montana? Why that small place? Her Mom came from Weeki Wachee, why not go there? I mean, if you want to be a mermaid then at least the water's warm and you get paid.

And that line on the map – in red. Eventually darker thoughts and fears crept into my mind. Was she going there to end it? She had seemed to be getting weaker, to be failing. Maybe being exposed to Rye had shown her too much, had pointed out what she could have been.

I couldn't tell, and I could mail letters but had no phone number, so I just imagined. And life kept on, and after a while I calmed down. Elena had been interesting, sure, a great swimmer and good person with a mysterious background. Not a mermaid, not crazy. But there were other thoughts in my head: things like what if we are different, or decide to be different... how much can we really remake ourselves? People can make themselves walk on fire, so what else can they do?

Life was busy busy busy. My letters stopped after seven months. I didn't hold anything against Elena for not answering; after all, she'd wanted time to be alone and think. And she took plenty of time, and moved on, I hoped. One night I woke up from a dream, a night-thought of what fifth grade science had taught us: that some insects create a chrysalis, a safe place to metamorph.

*   *   *

Eight months after I said goodbye to Elena I left the Holiday Inn and crossed town to the Hampton, became the housekeeping manager. A pretty small thing if you look at all the things a person could make of themselves. But it pays the bills, and I like running a department. I work four ten hour days and three off, so I have time to work on... well, other things. I met a decent guy – after trying the car repairman for a while – and that worked out well.

A year and a month went by. And then, like it happens in stories and movies, a letter came to me, forwarded over from the Holiday Inn. It was from Elena, of course. It was postmarked Ogunquit, Maine, and before I even opened it I had to look up Ogunquit. Right on the Atlantic coast. I had to admit I was glad she was alive.

There was just a single page inside, written in her quick flowing style, the letters like waves on the paper.

*Marcie:*

*I hope you're well. It's been a long time, and I have thought about you quite a lot. You were always a good friend. You helped me through some tough things, and I think it's helped me move on to something better.*

*Montana gave me time to... pull in, I guess. To really think, and find what it was I needed to do. Anyway, there are a lot of things we could catch up on. I would love for you to visit, whenever you like. I know it's a long way to travel so I fully understand if you cannot.*

*I really hope you can visit. Let me know.*

*But I promise I did not grow a tail, or gills.*

*Elena*

Ogunquit, Maine. I laughed at the idea, but in all honesty, I really wanted to see Elena. I had the time off due and some money saved, so I asked the General Manager, and he said that would be fine. The only catch was it would have to be in the slow season, in January.

# 16

So I flew to Maine in the middle of winter. There wasn't a lot of snow that month but it was brutally cold. Elena met me at the airport, and I could tell right away that she was better. She was happy, and glowing like she'd stood in rain for a year.

And back at her apartment – a nice, small, and still barely furnished place – she slid off her coat and sweater and I could see that she'd filled out. No, more than that – I was awed, really, and couldn't help but stare. It was the same woman, but twice as much: the line and form of her body was smooth and taut, filled with muscle. No ripples and muscle-piled-on-muscle look, but incredibly healthy and solid. She was only a few inches taller than me and not much more in dress size, but I had a feeling she could be twice my weight. And she radiated energy like an electric heater.

We spent a few days together, wandering the city, talking about work (she had a job near the water, some kind of dockworker), normal things. She had no current boyfriend and no tail, no gills. It was a good time and good talk, in-depth friend talk but I won't go over all of the laughs and chatter.

Because everything about that visit, about Elena, came down to the last night. She had been growing a bit tense during my stay. Not in a negative way, but as if she was expecting something, or looking forward to something that still made her nervous. And she'd been holding back, that was obvious to us both.

We'd spent the visit like I said, mostly in Portland or a few places inland, and we'd only been near the water when she showed me where she worked, which was fine, it being so cold and icy.

I was due to fly out early on Tuesday, and Monday night we ate at her place. After we cleaned up she told me to dress warm, lots of layers. She wanted to show me something she'd been holding for a surprise. I told her that if it was out in that freezing air at night she could forget it.

"I'm sorry," she smiled, and rubbed my shoulder a bit. "Really I am, but you know, in these last few days, we never talked about how things ended up... with me."

"We didn't?" I said, confused. Did we have too? I mean, she had a job and a place and was happy, what else was there? Of course she wouldn't say any more, just took me to her old truck.

We drove a bit, to a place called Two Lights Park. It was a small rocky point over the dark and cold ocean; there was enough moon to see the bright chunks of ice on the rocks, and the foam of the waves below. The wind had stopped and it was incredibly cold, but I had to admit it was beautiful.

We walked up onto the rocks a bit. "Thank you," I said to Elena, over my shoulder. I could see why she'd gained so much strength here: being this close to the ocean, feeling the salt air and hearing the surf must have helped a lot. "I'm freezing my ass off but it is beautiful."

And that was it. I'm sorry, if you heard me tell this a thousand times you'd still hear my voice catch. That was it: I told Elena it was beautiful, and when she didn't answer I turned around, and saw her standing silent on a flat stretch of rock, her bare skin nearly luminescent in the moonlight, her clothes a heap at her feet. She looked once at me, her eyes incredibly wide and dark, and she smiled from some far-gone depth.

And then with an incredible silent speed she left me and the moonlight and the rock behind, leaping out and into the ocean.

## EPILOGUE

*Elena could perceive the exact second the tide turned.*

*It now rose and shifted inward, a whisper of increasing surf and a thin rattle of cobbled rocks as the water drained from the Maine coast, returning – for the moment – to the night sea.*

*A sliver of waning moon began to edge over the distant horizon, and a hair-thin touch of pale light grew along the water. Minutes passed, until the moonlight reached the sand and stone, crept along the cliff-top, and fell against the woman standing at the edge of the salt-stained rocks. She remained silent, vague in the blue-gray light: only a faint shifting of black eyes following the roll and break of waves betrayed an alert attention.*

*She was calmed here, settled not only by the slightly phosphorescent foam and the smell of salt, but by the sound, intimate to Elena since her long-ago birth... a sound that called to her constantly and echoed through her days.*

*Elena Constance McLayne walked behind her friend, following her across cold smooth stone and rubbery seaweed until she could feel the foaming border where ocean slid onto earth.*

*Her friend pulled her coat tight and close, and Elena saw the gesture,* appreciated the time and effort made. It was this friend, after all, who had coaxed and prodded Elena to this point.

Elena waited as the wave slid back out, then eased a foot onto a small patch of wet rock. Only the slightest bit of salty moisture contacted her body – a tease, really – but even that was enough to break the temporal hold and provide a glimpse of renewed strengths.

Tremors ran through her legs as her body anticipated the pleasure and power to come. "A miracle..." she murmured. Chemistry came to mind, the terms and formulas of a dozen books and classes from across the years.

Water is a miracle, even in a sterile state. It is the only substance that will freeze into a less dense mass, enabling it to float on a lake or river... thus protecting unfrozen water beneath... thus protecting aquatic life, the progenitor of human life. Terms and formulas for an ancient power. Water is neutral in pH, stable, transparent, allowing aquatic life to survive. It is The Universal Solvent.

But then, then... take that water and add salt and scores of minerals of earth's eons... add tide and current and wave, life and force...

Elena paused, as she always did, allowing the faintest scent of salt and minerals and ancient water to embrace her senses. And the union was made, the relationship opened once more. With her inner eye she could see the tide turning toward high, the exact water temperature, the salinity rich and welcoming, currents calling... to far deep places... already she could hear the ocean, hear the song she'd been born into. The low rumbling tide, ancient deeps, the high whisper of roiling curls.

A measured step forward, then two – she paused at the point where the water's music could no longer be denied. Her eyes were closed but she could feel the approach of each roller, knew the exact instant each would curl and break; eyes shut, she could still see the largest wave approach, dark, and potent.

Then Elena slipped from the remainder of her clothing, took two light steps over scattered chunks of ice – and leapt into the dark January waters of the Atlantic.

# FOUR DEGREES

## BY TIMOTHY LYNCH

**Orlando, Florida  19-Dec-2035**

"Well, we'll be in the double-o's again with lows in the low 90's. Go to the mountains or the woods or the beach and bring along lots of cool drinks. How about you, Shannon? What do you do to keep cool?"

"I think I might park myself right under my air conditioning."

"That sounds perfect! Remember the sunscreen for the kiddies folks, and plenty of water for your pets. Remember too, to use the misting stations available at all public buildings. You know, scientists say we're on track for a global increase of four degrees. So keep practicing your warm weather safety tips."

**Maine Woods  24-Jun-2036**

A green SUV with State of Maine insignia on the doors slowly drove up the trail. When the deep treaded tires stopped, a green-khakied Marc Blaque exited the truck. Palming the branches away from his face, his boot heels dug up moss and lichen leaving deep scars in the hillside as he made his way down the steep bank. Broad hands gripped the base of grass clumps controlling his descent. He didn't want to make trouble for the sportsmen but every now and again he wanted to know what they were *really* up to.

Below, the early June babble of a wide stream hid the sounds of the forest. But even from twenty yards he could hear the sharp whir of casting and the chatter of humans. Marc headed further upstream toward Beaver Trail and Brandy Bridge. From there, he would make his way downstream on the opposite side of the bank.

The trail was wet from rain, but he nimbly hopped from root, to dry spot, to fallen tree branch, circumventing the worst muddy spots. As he stood on the branch, he remembered a few choice falls: one time his boot sank so far into the mud all he had left was his sock. He had watched as the hole filled with water, turned and headed back to his truck.

Brandy Bridge had the usual sightings of "albino hairless seals" jumping from the rocks. They hid under the water or grabbed their towels when they saw Marc's uniform. He thought they looked fairly young, so he yelled down, "Put your bathing suits back on, I'll be back in ten minutes!" He was certain they'd be gone by the time he returned. He shook his head and thought of his own two little girls. *Please give me ten more years before I have to worry about that stuff.*

As he walked the other side of the bank, the trees thickened and the path rose. A muffled quiet surrounded him. A sunny break in the trees gave him a good view of the stream. Marc caught movement from the corner of his eye. A quick turn rewarded him as he witnessed the biggest eagle he'd ever seen pluck a huge fish from the surface of the water, flying away with it flapping in his talons.

**Near Point Hope, Alaska  12-Jan-2038**

Uglu pulled on the ice-covered wire bobbing up and down. Sea water sloshed around the edges of the fishing hole as the barge of ice they floated on rode the unquiet sound. Even winter ice in the arctic was perilous now that temperatures had risen over the years. Great hooks and cables held ice-floats near to shore, preserving the Inuit family's life of fishing and hunting whale. Now that most of the true polar bears were gone, that was one less thing to worry about on the ice. Uglu looked over with envy at the two fish tails peeking above his brother's bucket, then gripped his own lifeless wire with his seal skin mitten, giving it a tug or two. Uglu's father called for the boys to pick up.

Uglu gripped the front-edge of the wooden sled. The three went out farther onto the ice.

Here, near the claw-toothed hooks that held the ice, thinner ice sheets buckled after repeatedly crashing together then refreezing, leaving frozen ramps and scars. Uglu's father tested the ice with his weight. No movement. He waved his sons forward. Uglu's hand-drill scraped the hard ice surface, biting and grinding. Uglu's father walked the camping lantern out as far as he dared then set it down and returned to their wooden sled. Uglu drilled his brother's fishing hole much closer to his own. Uglu's father gave each of his boys a hunk of fat to chew, then picked up the drill for his own fishing hole. Uglu added some fresh slippery squid to his hook then watched it sink into the black water.

The wind ruffled the fur on Uglu's hood as he listened to the squeaking of the ice sheets. Then, suddenly, a great thud.

Sound reverberated through the ice and the foam pad on which he sat. The sled jumped a few inches and the camp lantern fell over. Uglu's father grabbed the emergency spotlight from the sled, lighting up the ice. Nothing.

Then the camp lantern rolled and flipped. Uglu's father focused the 30,000 candlelight spotlight on a massive black and white head. Uglu's father waved his arms and cursed at the orca as the campfire lamp disappeared beneath the shining black eye.

## Chihuahua, Mexico  03-Mar-2038

Juanita Martinez struggled to put on some "musica buena" from the old CD player her son Manuel bought her. She was terrified it would break and then her music would be gone. She knew her son couldn't buy her expensive electronics, and her dear friends had given her such beautiful CD's over the years. She danced the dances she knew all her life, perhaps with less vigor, but they always made her feel wonderful. Her music was her life except for her son and her two cats. Angelina, a lean black and white, with the most beautiful brown eyes, walked on the top of the sofa. "¿Tu bailas conmigo Angelina?" she coaxed.

Lobo, her other cat, named for the tuft of grey hair that stood up on his back when he was "gato gruñon" was nowhere to be found, usually appearing when she opened a can of food. She looked at the clock, remembering her son would be by to check on her during his lunch break. She danced to the kitchen then opened her sparse cupboard for a can of beans. The piercing of the can brought Lobo sprinting to his dish, waiting and meowing loudly.

"¡No es para tí, Lobo! Es para Manuel." Lobo seemed to understand her words and meowed even louder.

When Manuel opened the door to check on his mother, she was backed in a corner, her hands bleeding from scratches from Lobo's claws. Angelina licked crushed beans from her paws as she stepped over an overturned pan. The grey tuft on Lobo's back rose with every hiss.


## Outside Lincoln, Nebraska  26-May-2039

Janice Stone reclined on the porch. She turned the page of her latest romance novel. She was slightly disappointed in the main love interest. He was muscular with dark hair and grey eyes. Handsome enough, but she liked her guys with lean bodies and sandy blond hair. She clicked ahead to see if any blond boys were coming up in later chapters. She shrugged. No luck, only the women were blondes. "Dammit, Cheryl," she said, looking directly at the author's name. She tossed her compu-glasses on the wicker chair in front of her and got up to get some lemonade from the fridge.

The heat in the house was unbearable, so she opened the freezer to stand in the frosty air for a few seconds before grasping a plastic tray and giving it a twist. The sharp edged cubes tumbled into her glass. She opened the fridge and pulled out her cool, tart lemonade and poured the last of a two-liter jug into the glass.

She returned to the porch to a surprise. A large grey-brown rabbit crouched under her coffee table, trembling.

"What's the matter, bunny?" she said.

When she approached, the rabbit darted from one corner of the porch to the other.

"You must be lost! You can stay here if you want. I won't hurt you," she cooed. As she lay back down, the rabbit sat near a potted plant. Janice couldn't help herself. She sat up and slowly approached the frightened rabbit once more. She gave the rabbit plenty of room, since it was shaking so. It was then she heard growling and looked at the field across the street. Five big coyotes were shoulder-deep digging up the field. Dirt flew in all directions as powerful front paws ripped at the earth. What looked to be a savage male stopped digging only long enough to snap at his pack-mates, if they dared get too close. She watched and listened to the canine donnybrook for a minute, then looked down at the rabbit, "Bunny, you need to dig deeper holes!"

## Medford, Oregon  17-Apr-2040

Bill Hooks switched on the helicopter blades and radioed fire control that he was thirty minutes out. The sun wasn't even close to coming up yet. The slow churning twin blades quickened until a man-made cyclone spun dirt and dust into clouds. He pulled up and heard the blades rip at the air with a low groan. The huge Chinook gained altitude and tipped to the west. *This is the fifth fire in two days*, Bill thought as he raced over the trees. *The Service does a good job clearing brush, but dry is dry. One day science will figure a way to neutralize the lightning*, he thought. *Then we'll only have rain. All of the good, none of the bad. A decade ago 200,000 acres would burn before we got it under control. Not today. Today we actually save people's houses.*

*They might smell some smoke but that's about it.*

Bill saw a glow in the distance and radioed to see if his "shadows" were on the scene. Mike and Stu usually beat him to the fire, but he was the flight chief. The tanks didn't open till he said so. "Finally!" Lights panned the horizon ahead. He reached for his com. "Morning boys. Let's do this." The three huge helicopters lined up over a hot spot, touching their metallic bellies to the treeline. "Lights out, boys!" Bill's signal allowed nine tons of frosty liquid nitrogen to charge down the mountain, snuffing out every bit of heat in its path.

### Santa Cruz, California  05-May-2040

Dr. Susan Soffet pushed open the glass doors to Stein Hall. In her pocket she carried a portable drive with labs to grade and some downloaded science articles to add to her lab wall. Several beads of sweat ran between her shoulder blades as she mentally organized the day's itinerary. She would check on just over two hundred cultures maturing from her BIO 107 classes, start writing a forward for her colleague's new book in genetics, and if she had time, her *own* work. A swipe of her hand retracted the electric locks with the sound of large snapping fingers. Inside the lab, a few tired grad students worked on DNA samples and protein analysis, as her low heels clicked toward the back of the room. She uploaded the articles to the display wall and placed a "New!" graphic on each one. On her office door hung a note from a student who was failing her BIO 100 course. *Did he think a plea on paper would make a difference?* She waved her hand again and waited for the lock's soft click.

The sun beamed through her office but a dark spot on the wall caught her eye. *Wolf spider? No, too compact. Jumping spider?* She took a few steps closer. *Yes. Zebra spider? What have you been eating?* Susan walked across the room to pick up a one liter beaker, brushing the spider into the container with a pencil. "Well look at you," she said, snapping on the lid. "You just became my new project!" A quick visit to a colleague's reference site showed measurements of arachnids in California.

"It says here you should be no larger than six or seven millimeters." Taking a ruler out of her desk, she held it under the beaker. "So why are you almost twelve?"


## Madison, Wisconsin  28-Jan-2041

"Is the witness ready? Good. Very well. This opens the Public Hearing of The State of Wisconsin concerning WholeWheat. Keep in mind, this proceeding is not a trial but simply a fact-finding mission. Mr. David Samuelson is here today on behalf of The WholeWheat Agroprizes Corporation to answer questions concerning the genetically-modified–"

"Mr. Speaker, WholeWheat Agroprizes takes issue with the term 'genetically-modified.' We prefer the term 'enhanced.' "

"Genetically-enhanced–"

"Just 'enhanced,' Mr. Speaker. We further ask that the record reflect that change."

"Without exception... Ms. O'Connor?"

"Does WholeWheat Agroprizes deny that the product WholeWheat is genetically-modified?"

"WholeWheat Agroprizes simply requires its copyright and patent associations to be clear. The WholeWheat product may, by law, be associated with the term 'enhanced.' With all due respect, Mr. Speaker, WholeWheat Agroprizes asks that any and all terms beginning with or including the letters g-e-n-e in succession be stricken from the record. WholeWheat Agroprizes can and will exercise legal action to ensure its brand."

"Auspicious beginnings," mumbled the speaker sarcastically. "Does the witness wish to make a statement for the record?"

"Thank you, Mr. Speaker."


## North of Lake Pontchartrain, Louisiana  20-Mar-2045

J.J. Weeks followed the low river, flipping over stones looking for crawdads to sell at the nearby campground. Today, he thought he'd try further downstream where the water slowed and there were some deeper pools. The wide shallow river was his prime hunting ground.

He put the small net in the water behind the crawdad, hopefully before it realized it was found. *Damn, do they ever take-off once they see you*. He sold the small ones for small-hook fishing. Big ones could either be eaten or pawned off on dumber sportsman as "the way to catch bigger fish." As usual his buckets were filling fast, though the crawdads weren't standing still or jumping into the net. J.J. was just good at catching them. His shorts were soaked up to his crotch and his shoulders were sunburned and it was only 10 A.M.

J.J. waded toward shore. He would step down, wait for the rocks to slip, then step down again with his full weight. In this way, he made his way across the shallow river. He was almost to shore when he noticed a big flat rock completely undisturbed. He readied his net where he guessed the crawdad's tail might be and plunged his arm into the cool water. He lifted the rock slowly, hoping not to stir up too much silt. Mud-mist covered the space under the rock and he watched as the current moved away the silt. J.J. let go of the rock and jumped backward, falling into the stream. Two hand-sized claws opened wide in warning.

## Coastal Hong Kong  8-Aug-2047

Portia Matthews crossed her legs and bit the end of her pen, waiting for the CEO to come into the conference room. Her colleagues sat behind their nectars and teas, while she added a slice of lemon to her water. She twisted in her chair to glance at the now flooded Hong Kong skyline. Waves lapped at abandoned first floor windows.

A six-foot-ten Swedish suit and tie strode in like he just got off an elliptical. His secretary followed with a cart of blue packets.

"This year we have a new and exciting campaign," he said in a light Swedish accent. "I have one word!" He reached down and pressed a button under the massive mahogany table.

From the back of the room double doors burst open on two shining silver carts. On each several plates sizzled and popped.

"Bacon!"

A few people cheered, as the assistant passed out the packets, but Portia remained quiet and raised her hand. "Haven't we done bacon? There's bacon ice cream and bacon salad, soy bacon, and bacon vodka along with all the breakfast fare."

Full blond brows made Anders Ingolf look angrier than he really was. "All the same, people, we have to get ahead of this. All the major companies are doing it, and so will we! I feel it's perfect for our economy line. As it says in your packets, 'We have not begun to explore this option.' Keep in mind, this is just for Home and Beauty. We'll produce bacon shampoo, bacon de-odorant, bacon lip gloss, bacon toothpaste, you name it. It's an exciting new campaign! Now everyone turn to the top of page five."

### Odessa, Ukraine 30-Apr-2048

Ivana gripped air, not the waiting hands of her partner hanging inverted on his trapeze bar. She cartwheeled downward into the safety of the net. Bouncing twice, she felt the grip of the ropes. She grabbed the outer edge of the net and flipped down to her feet. Setting her hands and feet on the small ladder rungs that protruded from the steel pole, she climbed upward, back to heights from which she fell. As she climbed, she heard the cheers of the crowd, and the voice of the ringmaster introducing the next act.

Crack.

The lion tamer's whip snapped. Cheers erupted from the crowd. Crack, crack. Ivana heard the roar of the lions, then more cheers and screams.

She went over the flips in her head. *Did she reach out to Bruno too soon?* At the top of the ladder, she put her hand out for some help but no one helped her. Their heads were pointed down, watching the act with as much enthusiasm as the audience.

"Bruno! Here!"

Her partner grabbed her arm like a vise, lifting her onto the platform. She heard more screams rising, falling and then rising again. She heard gunfire.

She looked down at the crowd leaping from the stands and rushing to the exits.

A tiger dragged the lion tamer by his neck. Two lions mauled a polka-dot suit with big floppy shoes.


## Potsdam, New York 15-Aug-2048

Jake Hayes balanced a thirty aught-six on the rail of his deck and put his eye to the scope. Things were looking up since he realized the bears that came through his yard weren't the nuisance he first thought. A clean bear skin could fetch five hundred dollars on a bad day, depending on the size and where he put the bullet. He never imagined the expansive dump on the next property could be such a boon. It was almost too easy. An absolute giant male stood up on its hind quarters, looked in his direction, then quickly darted across the lawn.

"Do that again, I dare ya!"

He reached for a plate of crackers with sardines and cream cheese, carefully bringing the hors d'oeuvre to his lips. "The only way to hunt!" His teeth crunched down on the salty treat. He took a good-sized swallow from his cold beer and slowly sighted the perimeter of the lawn, looking for large dark shadows.

"There." A large black female lumbered at the edge of his yard. "There." Another male in the trees to his right.

"Now, who will give me the best shot?" He heard an odd thumping behind him. Then the plate glass window exploded.


## St. Catharines, Ontario 9-May-2050

Sean Temers checked the camera view outside his home. All clear – wait, was that something around the neighbor's garage? He waited another five minutes then checked again. He opened the reinforced steel door and ran the ten yards to his car. Slamming the car door shut, he nervously turned the key and pressed the start button. The engine revved and he threw the car into drive. He checked the battery, about two-thirds full. *Good. All I need now is a close parking spot at work.*

His drive was uneventful. He noticed a few dogs, and a raccoon on the way, but nothing attacked the car. He pulled into a very quiet parking lot.

"Dammit!"

All the prime spots were taken; the fire-lane was full too. Cars on the outskirts were parked, blocking others in.

"This is bullshit!" He drove around the building looking for a way in. A service entrance. *Totally full. Come on, come on. Ha, somebody parked on the opposite side of the building from the doors... Good luck dodging anything from there! Dead man walkin'... 'Course he wouldn't have to wait for anybody to leave... no, no. Too risky!*

He turned the next corner. There was an entrance near a trash receptacle.

"Yes, only two cars!" *Looks like I'll be partnering a getaway with a tannish Prius, ZZD. Should be easy to find. I'll send an urgent email.*

Sean checked his front, back, and side cameras. *Clear.* He opened his door to get out. Closing the door gently, he made sure that the car doors were unlocked and started for the front of the office building. *Not too fast, not too slow. Not too fast, not too slow. Don't attract attention. Good.*

Ahead, the armed guard saw his approach and opened the gate. He relaxed when he saw the guard wave to let him in. The guard brushed something about the size of a nickel off of his arm.

"Don't worry, Bud. Just a tick." Flipping itself over, the tick began to crawl back toward its host. The guard brought the edge of his boot down hard. Sean heard the tick's body break like a potato chip.

## Scranton, Pennsylvania  2-Sep-2051

The Pennsylvania National Guard was taking action. Each state had their orders from Washington, D.C. There had been too many fatalities nationwide and people were frightened to even go to the store for groceries. The added bait of a full complement of fruits, vegetables and treats to go with the flesh of a shopper brought numerous species of four-legged killers slinking between parked cars, ready for ambush.

But now that would all change. No more scary parking lots and trips to the shed. Finally, they had a plan. Hundreds of heavily armed guardsmen fanned out in a 360-degree push, followed by Bradley's and M2's with barrels trained on anything that moved. The tanks were followed by heavy equipment operators placing temporary Jersey barriers and walls of quick-drying cement, separating the city from the wild. Once the perimeter was established, they'd go out again to reinforce the wall with steel and more concrete. It would just be a matter of time before people could live in peace again.

Little Janey Andrews watched the vehicles moving away. Her father had his hand on her shoulder and everyone was really excited. "No more mean animals," her father had told her. She thought of things to do when the wall was finished. *There would be so many more places to play*, she thought. Janey looked down at her arm where two bulbous abdomens were filling with blood.

"Get them off, Daddy! Get them off!"

Her father slapped twice at her arm, splattering her face and dress with blood.

# 'ROSE IN DREAMS
## BY RICHARD VEYSEY

**H**ave you ever had a dream that felt like it was totally real?"
Jerome took a bite of his pizza. As always, the school cafeteria's
food barely passed as edible.

"I have them sometimes," Chastity replied. "They're very surreal. I usually freak out and wake myself up."

"Did you have a dream like that last night, Jerome?" Aiden asked.

"Yeah. My brother had a nightmare and came into my room. When we
fell asleep, we had the same dream. We were in my bedroom, then we decided to go downstairs, and suddenly we were in the kitchen."

"That was his first nightmare in a while, ever since your dad yelled at him, right?" Aiden asked, handing his pizza crust to Jerome. Aiden was a slender boy. He rarely finished everything at lunch, so he gave what he didn't eat to his friends.

"Yeah. I think he was more scared of our dad than of the things in his nightmares. You know how scary my dad can be. He must be even scarier to a three-year-old."

"Didn't he spank Chris with a ruler for running out into the woods with Fluffy last week?" Chastity asked. She scratched at the top of her head, then pushed her dark, curly hair back into place.

"Yeah, and he did the same to me for other things when I was a kid. I'm glad Chris is better than me. I think my ass probably had callouses on it because of how often he punished me."

Chastity and Aiden chuckled quietly. The three of them continued to eat in silence.

"So you had a 'lucid dream,' right? Was this your first?" Aiden asked.

"A lucid dream? What's that?"

"It's when you have complete control over the things that happen in your dreams. I've heard that a person can learn to make all their dreams lucid and live out fantasies while they sleep."

"I wish I could do that," Chastity said, "I know exactly what I'd dream about every night."

"You'd be spending every night with Charlie, wouldn't you?" Aiden teased, puckering his lips and making exaggerated kissing noises.

"Shut up!" Chastity blushed.

"In your dreams," Jerome smiled. "And not like those dreams would be particularly steamy, anyways. You freak out when a guy even tries to kiss you."

"No. Oh no." Chastity glared at Jerome. "Don't you go there. I didn't like Harry. It was just a dance, and I wasn't ready for it. If it had been Charlie–"

"You don't have to make excuses," Aiden said. "Some of the girls at that dance were all over every guy they danced with. That's just gross."

"Well, everybody else seems to love them," Chastity sighed.

"All the guys love them because they know they can get laid," Jerome said. "And all the other girls just want to be friends with them so they can get some of that popularity for themselves. You're lucky. We like you because we think you're awesome."

Aiden nodded emphatically and wrapped an arm around her, giving her half a hug.

*    *    *

Jerome stood by his bed. It had taken him an hour to fall asleep. The talk of lucid dreaming at lunch had inspired him to attempt it again. Online many people said it took months, if not years, of training to master the art of lucid dreaming. Most said it was rare for someone with no experience to do it twice in a row. "Finally something I'm good at," Jerome said to himself.

"Am I seeing the real world right now?" Jerome thought out-loud. "No, this is a dream. I should be able to do anything."

The walls and ceiling, prompted by Jerome's imagination, fell outward, revealing a starry night sky above. He could see the trees surrounding his house, their leaves bright with the colors of autumn. A small shed, which stood a few feet from the side of his house and held various lawn supplies, remained untouched. He nodded and it vanished in a puff of smoke. With a wave of his hand the sky flipped, as if time had been sped up and the night had passed to day in a moment. Jerome admired the scene spread out before him. "Now what?"

He wished he could share this experience with Chris. His brother would love having the power to paint an entire world with his mind. "Perhaps it's possible," he said to himself. He focused again on his room, willing the world around him to return to reality. As the familiar scenery reformed around him, he traced a path in his mind to Chris's room.

Though Jerome had little doubt that the room was yet another illusion created in his brain, everything looked and felt so real that he found it hard to accept that he wasn't awake. His brother, or at least this mental representation of him, slept soundly. Jerome gently placed a hand upon the illusion's shoulder. "Chris, wake up. Chris?"

The boy in front of Jerome refused to move, even as Jerome shook him with increased force. "Of course he won't wake up," Jerome thought aloud. "This isn't really him. Maybe I still can find him, though."

This place was merely a construction in Jerome's mind, no more than a self-created fantasy world within which anything was possible. His brother existed somewhere outside.

Jerome focused on an empty space and found himself surrounded by darkness. He looked down at his hands, wondering at how he could see them without light, yet he realized that he wasn't 'seeing' anything: this was merely his mind's projection of the body he expected to have. With another surge of focus, he removed the image of his body from the dream world. Jerome felt uneasy, perhaps even queasy, with the complete lack of sensation. He forced himself to allow nothing to intrude into this space.

Before, the space had been three-dimensional, but now Jerome could almost imagine that it was a flat sheet of black paper. He knew that Chris was somewhere beyond that darkness. Holding on to the void, he focused on passing through it. He felt a strain in his mind similar to what he felt in his legs while running as he forced his way outside of the world within his mind.

Jerome sensed energy all around him, glowing and creating a luminescence that seemed completely opposite from the void he had just left. This was a light he could not dismiss, no matter how hard he tried. As he stopped holding on to the image of the void, other things began taking shape before him.

He felt the sensations of floating and moving swiftly forward. Below him was what appeared to be water. On the surface were long, dark patches interspersed with large spaces of bright, shifting color. He tried to turn to look above, but it was as if some force held his vision fixed to the water.

He reached his hand down, touching the dark surface below. He saw his hand pass below, yet felt no sensation of moisture. The water seemed to merge back together immediately behind him, forming no ripples and leaving no sign that it had been disturbed at all.

As his hand passed into the more colorful waters, his vision was filled with blurry, indistinct shapes and colors, as though he was looking at the world through the eyes of someone who desperately needed glasses. He slowed his motion, intrigued by the moving light show playing in his mind's-eye. It faded away as he passed back into darker waters again.

The ache in Jerome's mind had become an intense throbbing. He felt his hold on this world of water and color slipping, and his vision returned to darkness.

*   *   *

"So you had a dream where you were floating above water?" Aiden asked. "What's so special about that?"

Chastity's cat walked across the clean wooden floor of Chastity's room. She climbed into Aiden's lap, rubbing her head against his idle hands. Chastity moved closer to Aiden, reaching to pet the cat.

Jerome shook his head, "No, no, no. You aren't getting it. I was dreaming, and then I wasn't dreaming. It's like that film where the character realizes he's in a movie and goes into the real world."

"It doesn't make any sense," Chastity said, absentmindedly stroking her cat's fur. "First, there's no such thing as a hole in space that you can travel through and be somewhere totally different."

"Ever heard of black holes and worm holes?" Aiden asked.

"Well, kinda'." Chastity shrugged. Her hand grazed Aiden's. She looked up at him shyly, then slowly slid a few inches away from him. "But that's beside the point. Even if there were such a thing, if you're dreaming, you're dreaming; if you're awake, you're awake. You can't be both and you can't be neither."

"Unless you're dead," Aiden added quickly.

"Well, right," Chastity said, shooting a glare at Aiden.

"Guys, are you serious right now? I'm not joking around. It wasn't a dream, but I wasn't awake, either. It was like I was somewhere else entirely. I think I could get there again, tonight. Now that I know how, it shouldn't take as long and–"

"Okay, okay," Aiden interrupted, giving Jerome a reassuring pat on the back. "Can we talk about something else, now?"

*   *   *

Jerome floated above the water once more. Tonight it had only taken him seconds to enter the void of his dream world and pass through into this place. This time the colors were closer together and more distinct. He hovered above one of the lit sections of the water and dipped his hand in. He could make out some shapes. One looked like a man dressed in black. When Jerome focused on the figure, it gained further definition. He was almost certain that this was the priest at the church his family attended.

There was another figure in the room. This one was in a white robe. He focused on the figure and was able to make out the features of his father. The two men seemed to be having some sort of discussion, but the words sounded as if he was hearing them from several feet underwater. When he focused on their words, they became clearer. His father was debating some sort of religious point with the priest who was nodding and seemed to be losing the argument.

Jerome knew that his father went to sleep earlier than he did. He had no doubt that what he saw now was his father's dream. Feeling the fatigue creeping into his mind, he removed his hand from the water. There was more that he wanted to do here tonight.

He saw a bright light in the water a distance away. He drifted toward it and reached into the glow.

Colors surrounded him. Greens and blues and reds danced like the aurora. They twirled and intermingled, like hundreds of ribbons fluttering in an ever-shifting breeze. Through these colors Jerome occasionally caught the hint of shapes. Here a person, looking gigantic. There an action figure he vaguely recognized. Occasionally a puppy pranced into view, remaining longer than any of the other shapes.

Jerome smiled. These visions only confirmed what felt. This was his brother's dream. Unlike his father, Chris seemed to dream in ideas and emotions rather than in events. It was beautiful, but it would make finding the boy difficult.

As if cued by his thought of locating Chris, Jerome saw the ribbons stir and part. A small figure drifted toward Jerome. Even before his face was fully visible, there was no doubt in Jerome's mind that it was Chris.

Chris smiled. "Jerome! Do you want to play with me? Look at this toy Dad got me!" He reached through the ribbons, pulling a radio-controlled car from beyond them.

Jerome could feel the strain taking hold of his mind. "I don't think I have time. I can't stay here for long."

"Oh, okay," Chris pouted. "Why do you have to go?"

Jerome wanted to respond, to tell Chris that he didn't know why, but the darkness closed over him before he could say anything more.

*     *     *

"What are you doing this summer?" Aiden asked. He glanced at the clock, checking how much time they had remaining before the first class of the day.

"I haven't really thought about it," Jerome replied, "I think my mom wants me to go to that Catholic summer camp, again."

"Ugh, that sounds awful," Aiden replied.

"It's really not that bad. I'm not the only kid there whose parents practically forced them into going. I mean, I don't know if I really believe in all that Jesus, Mary, and Joseph stuff, but it's still kinda' fun."

"My mom says we're going to spend a month in Florida with her parents," Chastity said. "The beaches are nice, but it's really hot, and it's really not all that exciting down there."

"I'm a bit jealous," Aiden said. "I'll probably just be mowing lawns again."

"How much do you think–" Jerome began, then reconsidered his words. "Do you think you'll be able to save up much of it this year?"

"I don't know," Aiden said, smiling with his mouth, though his eyes looked sad and tired. "This year hasn't been easy for Dad and me. I think I'll need to help him out again, but there should be a little left for me."

"Oh," Jerome said absentmindedly. His interest in the conversation had reached an end. Recently, his excursions into the dream realm were all he could think about. Every day all he wanted to talk with his friends about was his experience the night before. Over the past three months he had tried on multiple occasions, but his friends couldn't accept that it was anything more than just a dream.

After his first time connecting with Chris, he had spent a month playing with his brother in a dream world they created together. Most of the first week was spent learning how to cooperatively shape that space. As the days passed, Jerome found himself able to stay in the dream state longer.

After the first month, the once large and indistinct spots of color in the water had become barely larger than his hand. For a month he simply spectated in the dreams of neighbors, each night traveling farther. The more distance he traveled, the quicker he became fatigued, but with each night his abilities grew.

"Jerome, are you coming?" Aiden asked. "The bell rang a minute ago. We need to get to class."

Jerome looked around. They were mostly alone in the cafeteria. "Oh, right," he said, standing, "I didn't even notice. I must have been really out of it."

"Are you okay?" Aiden asked. "You've been spacing out like that a lot lately. Chastity and I have been worried about you, especially with all these dreams you've been having."

"I'm fine. I've just had a lot on my mind recently."

"Okay. Well, you know we're both here for you if you need to talk."

*    *    *

Jerome turned out the light. Every night he tried to find Aiden and Chastity, yet each time his search ended in failure. He wanted to share this experience with them. He wanted them to believe that it was true.

It took him moments to arrive above the water. The lights below were the size of his palm. They spread out all around him, little clusters of lights glowing, becoming an aurora as they expanded into the distance.

He could travel several miles from his home, maybe even into the next town. Though he had watched hundreds of dreams, he was still afraid of interfering in any other than his brother's. His father would be angry and think he was practicing witchcraft. His mother wouldn't understand and would immediately talk to his father. Beyond his family, he almost thought people might shrug it off as nothing more than an unusual dream. But he wasn't ready to take that chance.

Jerome shivered as a tingling spread along his back, like he had emerged from cold water on a hot summer day. He turned and saw an unusual glow across the water. It started as a spot in the horizon and grew until he could imagine that the sun would soon rise there. Then it vanished.

In the three months since he had first found this dream realm he had never seen anything like this happen, and it frightened him. He began to turn away from where he had seen the light, but stopped partway and paused. After a momentary hesitation, he faced where the light had been.

Far in the distance, something stirred. A dark shape grew and spread, moving toward Jerome with increasing speed. As it drew nearer, its shape became more distinct. Black tendrils spread in all directions, probing the water below as if searching for something.

*   *   *

Jerome sat up in bed and looked out the window. The trees outside were illuminated by dim moonlight. Looking at the clock, he saw that it was shortly after 4 AM. He realized his heart was racing. He took a deep breath, forcing his body to relax.

No longer tired, Jerome got out of bed and began the trek to the kitchen. As he reached his doorway, his head began to tingle. He put a hand against the door frame, stumbling. He took another step. His vision blurred, then came back into focus. He slid his foot across the floor as he felt his legs tremble. His body pitched forward, his legs no longer supporting his weight. He was aware of a dull pain on his cheek as his vision turned to black.

"*What is this? A pool-user in the old world? How interesting.*"

"Who are you? What do you want?" Jerome cried into the darkness. He tried to move, but felt no sensation from his body.

"*I want to know how it is that you came to be here in the old world.*"

"The old world? I don't know what you're talking about."

"*What do you mean? Do you know nothing of Haven?*"

"No, I don't know what Haven is. Why are you–"

The voice in the darkness laughed. "*So you know nothing of the pool, then?*"

"Pool? What are you talking about?"

"*Ah, so they've forgotten. They don't remember the war. They don't re-member the pool. They don't remember anything. You've been most helpful–*"

Jerome felt tingling spreading across and through his brain.

"*Jerome. I think I have an idea in mind for you.*"

The tingling in Jerome's head turned into heat. It grew in intensity. Jerome tried to cry out in pain, but he made no sound.

"*What are you doing to that child?*" a woman's voice said. She sounded far away and distorted. "*Let him go at once!*"

"*Hmph, another pool-user?*" the voice in the darkness said. "*You can have him. I've done what I needed to do.*"

*   *   *

Jerome opened his eyes and looked around. He was lying on his bed. His mother, Roseanne, was sitting next to him, holding his hand.

Roseanne's eyes opened wide as she leaned toward him. "Oh, Jerome! I was so worried about you!"

"What happened?" Jerome asked.

"I don't know. I found you passed out on the floor ten minutes ago and called 911. They told me not to move you, but I'd already brought you to your bed." She put a hand on his forehead. "How are you feeling?"

"My head hurts."

"Did you bump it? I hope you don't have a concussion." Jerome's mother fidgeted. "I'm sure the paramedics will be here soon. They can check you out and make sure you're okay. I'm sure it's nothing serious."

"*Your doctors won't find anything.*" It sounded like the voice of the woman he had heard when he had been attacked.

"What? Who's there?" Jerome said, trying to look around the room, wincing with pain as he turned his head.

"*I'm not out there. I'm communicating with you telepathically.*"

Jerome's mother sat up, looking at him with wide eyes, "What do you mean? Are you hearing voices? Oh, if you're hallucinating that's not good at all. I'm going to get you some water. Stay there and don't go to sleep or move or anything." She stood and rushed off before Jerome could say anything to calm her worries.

"*You need to try to speak with me in your mind. Otherwise people will think you are talking to yourself.*"

'*Who is this?*' he thought.

"*I think you're trying, but I don't hear you. It's difficult to talk like this at first, but it's easy once you get the hang of it. Instead of just thinking words, try to think in a direction. Imagine your words being heard by me.*"

"*Okay. Can you hear me now?*"

"*Yes! You learn quickly. You have a natural talent for using the pool.*"

"'*The pool?*'"

"*Oh, how to explain it?*" The voice in his head paused. "*The pool is like a muscle, but it's in your mind. It can do things beyond your body, like communicate telepathically. You haven't been trained, so I'm sure there isn't much that you're able to do, but a well trained pool-user can do fantastic things.*"

"Here you are!" Roseanne walked briskly into the room, placing a glass of water on the bed stand next to Jerome. "Are you still feeling okay?

"Yeah, Mom, I'm fine."

"Do you need anything else? I already let the school know that you wouldn't be coming in today."

"No, Mom."

Roseanne stood by Jerome's bed, staring down at him with concern.

"Mom, could you leave?"

"Oh, right, sorry, hon. Just call me if you need anything."

Roseanne left as quickly as she had entered. Ordinarily she wouldn't have let his rude comment go unpunished. Whenever he was sick, though, Jerome could get away with saying or doing many things that normally would be told to his father.

"*You shouldn't be so rude to your mother,*" the voice chided.

"*I can talk to her how I want; she's my mother. Don't tell me what to do,*" Jerome replied.

"*I'm not trying to tell you what to do. Acting rude, though, is no way to make friends in life.*"

"*You're trying to tell me how to talk to my mom and I don't even know you. I find that pretty rude.*"

"*It was rude of me not to introduce myself. My name is Ageara.*"

"*Ageara? That's an unusual name. Where are you from? How are you speaking to me in my mind?*"

"*It's a long story, Jerome, and you'll have to just accept much of what I say as truth because I can't prove any of it to you. Hundreds of years ago–*"

"*Are you seriously about to give me a history lesson? Let's just skip to the important parts.*"

Jerome thought he sensed a sigh from Ageara. "*Fine. I'm not unfamiliar with the impatience of youth. Suffice it to say that I come from a place where abilities like our own are not uncommon. Though I do not have powers over dreams, I'm able to contact you telepathically, even when we aren't in the collective unconscious.*"

"*Okay, that's all great, but I'm more concerned about the evil tentacle monster that just violated my head. What was that? Why was it after me?*"

"*I was investigating it when it attacked you; I honestly still don't know what it is. When it sensed your presence, it immediately reached toward you. It seemed to be searching for those like us with the ability to use the pool.*"

"*That monster had consumed your projection before I rescued you. I don't know what it did to you, but I sense it left a mark on you. I've tried to sense the nature of that remnant, but it is elusive. The monster is far more powerful than any of the pool-users where I am from, even myself. For your sake, as well as for that of my people, I'm going to keep an eye on you."*

"*So there's something inside my head and you don't know what it is? Well, I feel great now. Tell me, since I'm sure my mom will want to know, is this something that will keep me from pursuing my education? Maybe it's not so bad if I get to stay home from school.*"

Jerome could imagine Ageara giving him a bemused smile. *"No, it's better if you act as if nothing has changed. It would be impossible for you to explain any of this to your friends and family. They haven't experienced what you have."*

"*So I'm just supposed to do nothing while I have this thing in my head?*"

"*I didn't say that we would do nothing. At night, while you are dreaming, I will help you train. There is much that you can still learn about using your gift, and perhaps along the way we can find the seed that the monster left inside of you. If we can find it, then perhaps we can destroy it."*

*     *     *

Jerome floated above the water. He had spent much of the day in the hospital. Roseanne and Chris had remained close by as the doctors tested him. After a few hours, they announced that they could find nothing wrong, advised Roseanne to give him plenty of water and for Jerome to go home and rest.

"*Ageara?*" Jerome called out.

"*Ah, there you are.*" He heard Ageara's voice clearly, though it sounded far away. He saw a speck appear on the horizon. It grew rapidly, indicating that it was moving faster than Jerome could comprehend. In moments, Ageara floated in front of him. Her voice and words had given him an impression of age, yet he was still surprised by the lines and wrinkles that covered her face. Her hair flowed down to her lower back, starting white near her skull with increasing black streaks toward the ends.

"*How do you move so quickly?*" Jerome asked.

*"I've had much more practice than you have. In a few years, you'll be able to move like that, too."* She smiled at him, *"I want to teach you some new abilities, but I need to know what you already have done."*

"Well, I'm here. I've gone into my brother's dreams and interacted with him. I've looked into other people's dreams. I think that's all."

*"You've made wonderful progress on your own, but there's much that I'll be able to teach you. Are you ready?"*

"I think so."

*     *     *

It had been a week since Jerome had met Ageara and begun his training. After their last session, Ageara had said proudly, *"You've come a long way. Tomorrow, I will teach you one of the hardest to learn skills for any dreamwalker. With the progress you've made this week, I think you're ready."*

Ageara would say no more on the subject, leaving Jerome full of curiosity. For the first time in months he struggled to fall asleep, kept awake by his excitement. When he finally found himself dreaming, he rushed to the collective unconscious, eager to see what Ageara had in mind.

When she arrived in front of Jerome, she wasted no time with pleasantries. *"Today I will teach you how to travel into the real world while you're asleep. It is a skill your society calls 'etheric-' or 'astral projection'. Are you ready?"*

Jerome had heard of astral projection before. Until today, he didn't even believe it was possible. *"Of course I'm ready!"*

Ageara chuckled. *"I'm glad you're excited. It's a very hard skill to learn, and it may take you months to master. First, I need you to return to your own dreamworld."*

Jerome nodded and sank into the water. He found himself in darkness. He still felt a momentary discomfort at the complete loss of sensation. He had to remind himself that it was all happening in his mind.

*"Now,"* Jerome could hear Ageara's voice, although it was fainter here. *"I*

*need you to imagine your room as it is now, with you in the bed. Accuracy is very important for a beginner."*

It wasn't hard for Jerome to bring his room into existence. He'd slept in the same room for most of his life, and saw all of its contents each night before falling asleep and each morning when he awoke. Imagining his own body on the bed was a more challenging task. When his form appeared, sleeping comfortably, Jerome felt an uncomfortable fluttering in his stomach.

*"Okay, Ageara. I've made my room. Now what should I do?"*

*"Now comes the most challenging part. You need to transition outside of your dream. Focus on staying in this state, but also allow yourself to awaken. It will help if you look at your body and will it to stay asleep. Does that make sense to you? It's hard to explain."*

*"I don't know if I understood that, but there's one way to find out."*

\* \* \*

Jerome sat up in bed. He cursed silently, realizing that he must have failed. He turned and looked at the clock. It was barely after 1 AM, giving him plenty of time to try again. With little effort, he slipped back into the dream world.

\* \* \*

Jerome stood in his imagined bedroom, staring down at his body again.

*"It's okay, Jerome. What you've done so far on your own has been impressive; don't worry if you can't succeed at this on your first try."*

*"Believe me, I've failed at many things before. I'm not going to beat myself up over this."*

Jerome looked down at his body. '*So, we meet again,*' he thought to himself. He clenched his fists tightly for a moment. '*This is my body. It is asleep on my bed, but my mind is awake here. I know that I can leave my body. I've done it before. I've been to my brother's dream. It's just like that.*'

The room around Jerome darkened. Dust particles floated through the air.

He looked at his body on the bed. There was a spot of drool on his pillow. He floated out of his room and up the stairs, finding himself by the door to his brother's room. Fluffy lay on the floor by his bedside.

The dog looked up when Jerome entered. He stared at Jerome, wagging his tail, but looking confused, like he wasn't sure what he was looking at.

*   *   *

Jerome reflected on what was probably the best time of his life. In the past month, he had spent much of his time practicing his gifts. At school, in the days before final exams, he traveled the school using etheric projection. He now knew what the girls' restroom looked like (though he couldn't bring himself to go into any of the stalls). He also knew that the school principal secretly watched TV when students and faculty weren't in the room, that teachers in the faculty lounge gossiped about students almost as much as the students themselves did, and that the cafeteria food was likely not fit for human consumption. Now that school was over, he had more time than ever to explore all the options his gifts gave him.

Yet the threat of the monster's seed inside his head was always present. It overshadowed any small victory and any joy he found in his accomplishments. Tonight, Ageara had told him, they were going to look for that seed.

Jerome slipped into the beyond. *"Ageara! I'm ready!"* he called across the water.

*"Good."* Her tone was more serious than Jerome had ever heard it. *"I need you to enter your dreamworld. That seed is buried somewhere deep in your mind. You may have to travel an unpleasant road if you're going to find it. Are you sure you're ready?"*

*"Considering the choice is this or waiting for something potentially awful to happen, yes."* Without waiting for a reply, Jerome slipped into the darkness.

*"So far, you have only tapped the surface of your mind. You have stayed within the level of the conscious, that which you have control over. The seed is somewhere deeper than that, somewhere in your unconscious. This will*

*not be easy, and unfortunately, the difficulty isn't going there, but being there. Do you ever have thoughts you can't control? Things you wish you didn't feel but still do?"*

*"Of course. Everyone does."*

*"Imagine them all brought to life in front of you. That is what you will be facing. These nightmares can hurt you if you let them, but your conscious mind will defend you. You can fight them. You will have to fight them if you want to find that seed."* Ageara paused, then continued slowly and with concern, *"You can always change your mind, if you want."*

*"I really don't like the sound of any of what you just said, but I'm not going to run away now."* Jerome heard a loud crack and felt a twinge in his brain. *"What was that?"*

*"What happened?"*

*"I don't know. I heard a noise and felt something in my head."*

*"It could be the seed! If you're going to find it, you have to go now."*

Jerome nodded, *"I'll be back, Ageara. I'll tell you all about what I find."*

Jerome created a field of roses. They were like the rosebushes his mother grew behind their house. He had always been comforted by those roses. *"Ageara, where am I supposed to go from here?"*

"Allow your subconscious into this conscious world. It will lead you deeper."

Jerome forced himself to lose focus on his world.

*"Jerome? Jerome?"*

Jerome looked around. In the distance he saw a silhouette. He sensed its eyes on him. *"Chris, is that you?"*

*"Follow me!"* The figure drifted backward.

Jerome hadn't noticed the rosebushes grow, but now they towered over him. Their shadows merged into a solid wall in the distance. The phantom of Chris joined with the darkness.

*"Remember, Jerome,"* Ageara's voice was like an echo from far away, *"These aren't real. They are only illusions. You give them power when you believe in them."*

Jerome stepped forward, following his brother's shadow. The roses towered above him, growing taller with each step. The darkness rushed to meet him.

*"Chris? Where are you?"* Jerome called out. He tried to illuminate the void, to fill it with something, but nothing happened. Here he was impotent.

*"Follow me!"* The voice was all around Jerome, giving him no guiding beacon. His eyes yearned for sight to give him a path. His ears yearned for sound to give him direction. His body yearned for sensation to tell him that he was moving at all.

*"I can't find you Chris! Help me!"*

*"Relying on a child to show you where to go? Isn't that pathetic."*

This voice came from no direction. It spoke into Jerome's mind from within. *"Who are you?"*

The voice chuckled, *"Who are you? Can you answer that question?"*

*"I'm Jerome."*

*"But what exactly* is *a 'Jerome'? What defines you? What makes you, 'you?'"*

*"I'm fourteen years old, I have a mother named Roseanne, a brother named Chris, a–"*

*"Stop, stop, stop. You're talking about numbers and other people. Is that all that gives you meaning? What if they didn't exist, who would you be then?"*

*"I-I-I'm just me. I'm myself."*

*"What can you do? What makes you any different from anyone else? What makes you special?"*

*"Dreams."* It was a new voice, faint, but close.

*"I have been to the world beyond dreams. I've gone into the dreams of others. I have this gift that is mine and mine alone."*

A ray of light shot from Jerome's chest, piercing the darkness. The luminous thread twisted off into the distance seemingly without end. He followed its path.

In the distance, he saw a lone figure walking toward him, matching his stride. Soon he could make out features: bright red hair, a shirt that seemed to drape over its body, a pale face riddled with red and white acne. He was close to Jerome's height, and with each step, the features gained more famil-iarity.

*"Look at yourself. Yes, that's you, Jerome. Aren't you hideous? Look at all those pimples! And have you ever gone outside? You're pale as a sheet. Look at your shoulders and your arms; there's no muscle, and you're practi-cally a post going straight up and down.*

"Nobody wants to look at you. Your voice is funny, too, so they don't even want to talk to you. Looking like that, you're going to go through your whole life alone. It's tragic, or it would be if there was anything you could do to change it. I guess since you can't, it's just pathetic. You're pathetic, Jerome. You're a waste of space, an ugly pimple on humanity, just like the ones on your face. Everyone's just waiting for you to go away and not bother them anymore."

Jerome collapsed onto the ground. *"No, please stop. Why are you saying these things?"*

"Because they're true. You know they're true or I wouldn't say them. You just don't want to know the truth. That's why I have to tell it to you. If you don't believe me, listen to your friends."

*"Look, it's Jerome,"* said Aiden's voice.

*"Indeed it is,"* said Chastity's voice.

*"What is he doing here?"*

*"I don't know. Maybe we should go someplace else? We don't need him around."*

*"Yeah, we're fine by ourselves. There's no reason we need to hang around his ugly mug."*

*"Stop, stop, STOP!"* Jerome cried out. He wanted to cry, but his eyes were dry.

*"Listen to him, sobbing over there,"* Aiden's voice said. *"What a baby. He doesn't have responsibilities like me. He probably couldn't even handle half of what I've suffered through, and I still have more generosity than him."*

*"Yeah, we're better off without him,"* Chastity's voice said. *"Anyways, I don't like how I catch him looking at me, sometimes. His eyes wander to my*

*chest more than I'm comfortable with."*

Jerome closed his eyes and wished it would go away. He wanted to be somewhere else, but didn't know how to find his way back, and he couldn't go forward. He started with alarm as he felt strong hands pick him up and carry him. Part of him screamed to struggle, to escape. He lay still, defeated, hopeless, alone.

*   *   *

Jerome opened his eyes. Multicolored light glowed around him. He tried to move but found his body paralyzed. He tried to scream but no voice emerged from his lungs.

*"Don't struggle, Jerome. There's really no point. Just watch and resign yourself to death."*

Jerome realized that he was still in the dreamworld. He tried to wake up, but the more he struggled, the more his head ached.

*"You can't get out of here. I've made sure of that. You're trapped here. You will slowly die as I feed off of your energy. I will grow stronger, you will grow weaker and eventually no longer exist."*

*"Who are you? Where am I?"* Jerome called to the voice in his mind.

*"I am you in a sense and yet, at the same time, I'm not you. Remember those cartoons you watched as a kid? Remember when someone made a moral choice, and the angel and devil would appear on their shoulder, representing their crisis of conscience? I'm that devil, or at least born from it.*

*"I've been incubating here, in the shell in which you are now trapped, feeding off of you, gaining self-awareness, free-will, and all those things that living beings most cherish. Now all that's left is for you to provide me with further power and a body."*

*"Please help me! Ageara!"* Jerome called out.

*"She can't hear you. Nobody can hear you while you're trapped here. There's no way for you to escape. You might as well abandon hope."*

*"I'm not going to give up fighting,"* Jerome spat.

*"Don't prolong your suffering. The more you struggle, the slower I feed.*

*Let me show you how hopeless you are. Watch. Not like you have a choice."*

Jerome's vision shifted. He floated above the water. His body moved faster than it ever had in the past. He settled over a light in the water and descended into another person's dream.

He emerged in a bright room full of people gathered in small groups, many talking to each other, their voices indistinct. At the center of the room a single figure sat in an elaborate chair, watching those assembled in the room. Every few moments, one of the others walked over to her and engaged her in conversation. She would smile gracefully and lovingly as she addressed them. Then, with a bow, they rejoined their group.

Jerome's feet brought him toward the center of the room. The crowd parted slightly for him. The attention of those in the room shifted from the seated figure to him.

Chastity smiled up at him from her chair. Though her face was recognizable, it was more slender and the lines flowed with more grace. Her eyes were slightly bigger, and her face had an unnaturally vivacious glow. Her normally curly black hair flowed straight behind her and sparkled in the bright light. "Oh, Jerome! I'm glad you could make it. Come, you can sit here next to me."

A chair appeared next to Chastity. Though smaller and not as elaborate as hers, it still had a regal quality. She gestured to it and frowned as Jerome remained on his feet before her. "What's wrong?"

Jerome's eyes took in the entirety of the room. "This dream is wrong. Look at all these people. They adore you. Is that what you desire? Don't you have enough love in the real world?"

"No! You know that. Nobody cares about me. Well, nobody except my family, you, and Aiden. I've never had a boyfriend. Guys don't even look at me. My figure is too round, my skin is too dark, my hair is too curly. Here I have respect and love."

"But this is just a dream. They love you because you demand it of them. Love has to be freely given or its not really love. The illusion you've created is just as quickly broken."

Jerome's body floated to the back of the room as the crowd returned its attention to Chastity. The assembled figures shambled forward, pieces of skin turning black and falling off. Their hair fell in clumps to the floor. Within moments, they had transformed into horrific creatures.

Chastity jumped from her seat and screamed. She stepped back slowly, then turned and ran.

"It's a shame. You made such a beautiful place, but there are no exits."

"Why are you doing this? What's happened to you, Jerome?"

"There is no Jerome anymore. He doesn't exist."

"Who are you?"

"I am Morpheus."

With a wave of Jerome's hand, the creatures vanished. Chastity huddled in the corner for a few moments before realizing that she was no longer in danger.

Jerome's feet took a few steps toward her, "You have been in the shadows for so long, wishing people thought you were beautiful and worth notice. You're a smart girl, and very compassionate. Yet you've always felt that your face and body have held you back. That doesn't seem fair, does it? All these other girls who are, let's face it, bitches, get all the attention that you deserve. And for what? Just because they're pretty on the outside?

"Haven't you wished that people's appearances reflected who they were inside? So that everyone could see that you were the truly pretty one and they were the ugly ones."

Chastity sank to her knees. She looked up at Jerome with blank eyes.

"No need to speak, just nod your head."

Chastity nodded slowly.

"So many people are obsessed with outward appearance. They won't even give you a chance if you aren't what society thinks is 'beautiful'. They don't even look at you. Their eyes just pass over you as if you weren't there. Don't you want to be looked at, seen, admired? Don't you want to be beautiful?"

Chastity was motionless. "Yes," she said, her voice barely above a whisper.

"Be glad, for making it so is no more difficult than uttering the words."

Jerome felt no sensation of movement, yet found himself standing by Chastity's side. "Now, let me give you what you desire." His hand lowered to her chin, then rose again, bringing her to her feet. With one swift motion, he grabbed the base of her skull and brought her face to his.

A warmth passed from his lips, down through his body. When he pulled away, Chastity's limp, withered form collapsed to the ground. "Farewell, Chastity. Rise, Lilith!"

The air in front of Jerome shimmered and began to take form. It solidified randomly, one piece at a time. Smooth, bronze skin appeared in patches, forming limbs and a naked female body. There was no flaw to be seen in her form, no complaint to be had. Jerome thought her features were shifting as he looked at her, that the color of her skin at times grew lighter or darker. The shape of a head appeared instantly. There were no lips, only a line indicating a mouth. There were neither nose nor ears. Her eyes were solid black ovals. She had no hair, neither on top of her head nor where eyelashes or eyebrows should be. She settled to the ground and looked up at Jerome.

He looked into Chastity's face, her familiar features restored. She smiled at him.

\* \* \*

"Jerome? Your alarm has been going off for ten minutes. Are you okay?"

Jerome felt his eyes open and saw his mother looking down at him with concern. He tried to move, to speak, but found that he could do neither.

"I'm not feeling so well today, mom."

"Again? Did you pass out? Should I call the doctor?"

"No, I'll be fine. I just might need to rest for a few days."

"Alright, honey. Well, let me know if you need anything." She set one of the handsets for the phone by his bed. "At least you don't have school, anymore." She gave him a pat on the arm and left the room.

\* \* \*

He wasn't sure how long he had been asleep when he heard the phone ring. His arm reached out and grabbed it. His finger answered it.

"Hello?" he heard his voice say into the phone.

"Jerome?" It was Aiden's voice. It sounded tired and hoarse.

"Yes. What's wrong?"

"It's Chastity. Her mom called me a few hours ago. She didn't wake up this morning, Jerome. They went to her room and found her and she wasn't moving. They took her to the hospital, but she wasn't breathing and she was dead." Jerome heard Aiden break into sobs. "Chastity is dead, Jerome."

His finger hung up the phone. His hand set it back on the bedside table.

"Oh, did you get the phone Jerome? Who was it?"

"It was just Aiden, mom."

"Oh, did he want to hang out? He must have been upset to hear that you're not feeling well. Maybe in a day or two you'll feel up to seeing him." She gave him an encouraging smile before leaving the room.

Jerome wanted to scream. He wanted to weep like he'd never wept before.

*    *    *

Jerome floated above the water. Morpheus had spent the day resting, forcing Jerome to do the same.

His mother had come to check on him often throughout the day and night, bringing him food and water that he didn't touch. He could feel a dull ache in his stomach, but couldn't eat or drink. His father came in once, and, later in the day, Chris had come and spent an hour playing by his bedside. Jerome could sense his brother's discomfort. Chris seemed aware that something was not right, even if he had no way of knowing what it was.

Jerome sank into the water. The room he found himself in was spacious and brightly lit. There was a family seated at a table. Jerome immediately recognized Aiden sitting between his father and a woman Jerome assumed was Aiden's mother. The table was small, yet the family sitting around it was close enough to leave plenty of vacant space.

"Can I hang out with my friends tomorrow, Mom?" Aiden asked excitedly.

"You always want to hang out with them," Aiden's father said.

"Oh, it's fine, Dale." Aiden's mother smiled. "You know how much he loves seeing Jerome and Chastity. They mean the world to him." She turned to her son. "Of course you can, dear. Let me know what your plans are and I'll drive you over to see them."

Jerome felt himself drawn forward and down, until he stood in front of the table.

Aiden and his parents turned toward Jerome, appearing pleasantly surprised.

"Oh, hey Jerome! It's good to see you!" Aiden grinned.

Jerome felt his feet bring him closer to his friend. His eyes moved across the room, taking in every detail. "In life you want for so much, yet here you have everything you could desire." His eyes settled on Aiden. "I'm here to give you a gift. But first, I want to show you something. Observe the frailty of dreams."

Aiden screamed as a bubble formed around him, trapping him. It appeared to be much like the shell in which Jerome was imprisoned.

"Your mother is dead in the real world, right, Aiden?" Jerome tried to fight against the force that moved him forward toward the frightened woman, who sat helpless in her chair. His mental struggle didn't even seem to slow his pace. With a single quick movement, Jerome's hands grabbed Aiden's mother's head and twisted until her face was aligned with her back. A loud crack preceded Aiden's high pitched, anguished wail. The body crumpled at Jerome's feet.

"Why?" Aiden sobbed.

"Don't worry, Aiden. It's just a dream." Jerome could feel his lips curve into an unwelcome smile.

Aiden's father stood and began running, but stopped mid-step. He looked at his inert feet as if confused.

"Hmmm, what to do with this one. Tell me, Aiden, how do you want your father to die?"

"Why are you doing this?" Aiden cried out.

"Because you're weak and far too kind, which is itself a weakness. You think only of giving to others, but never of yourself. We can talk about that more when we're alone, which brings me back to this." Jerome's arm gestured toward Dale. "Now, what should I do with him? Something quick, or something slow? It's not an easy choice to make, is it?"

"It's just a dream, it's just a dream." Aiden's eyes were closed.

"So you don't care? I'll make it something slow, then."

A clear cube appeared around Aiden's father. He put his hands on the side of the glass, facing toward Aiden.

"That cube is completely airtight. In a few moments, the oxygen level inside will become very low, and your father will struggle to breathe. Watch."

Aiden's eyes shot open unnaturally, as if forced. He appeared to struggle to turn away. He collapsed to the ground, his head facing forward as if supported by an invisible thread.

Jerome saw Dale fall forward onto his knees, his mouth open. Loud gasping sounds echoed through the kitchen.

"Now comes the best part. There is no longer enough oxygen in that chamber for him to survive. No matter how hard he struggles to breathe, he will feel himself starved of air. In moments, he will die."

Jerome wished he could look away as his friend's father died in front of him, but he was a prisoner behind his own eyes.

The walls fell outward around them. The furniture and decorations melted away. They were left standing on what appeared to be black, reptilian scales. There was no source of light in the sky, yet the air held the hazy half-light of a full moon night.

"Aiden, you have spent your whole life giving to others and having nothing for yourself. Your mother passed away when you were quite young, and your father coped in ways that weren't entirely healthy for his body or his wallet. You always had the power to keep that which was rightfully yours, yet you constantly gave, sacrificing of yourself for the well-being of others.

"But you knew, deep down, that you could use that money, those things better than others could, didn't you?"

"No," Aiden said, his voice flat. Tears ran down his face, but he didn't seem aware of them, "I didn't want anything."

"Now, now, no need to lie to me. We're alone here. I'm sure there were things that you wanted. Judging by your dream, I'd say you had quite large desires. Better food, a better house, a better life. You could have had those things, but everyone else, even people who had it better than you, were always asking you to give them what little you had. Do you know why it was always you that they asked?"

"No."

"Because they knew that you would say 'yes.' That's it. You were easy prey. You are generous. You are weak. Is that what you want to be?"

Aiden shook his head. "No."

"You want to be strong, right?"

Aiden nodded. "Yes."

"You want to have things of your own? All the things you have ever wanted and more?"

Aiden nodded again, this time not speaking.

"You can have that, if you want. You can have everything your heart could desire. People would respect you. They would give things to you. Do you want that? Come to me."

Aiden slowly stood, his legs shaking. He took a single hesitant step toward Jerome.

"No need to be hesitant. This is what you want, right? Come forward and seize it!"

Aiden increased his pace, stopping an arm's-length from where Jerome stood.

"Very good. Now hold still. This will only hurt for a moment." Jerome's body moved toward Aiden with unnatural speed. His hand grabbed his friend's hair, and he felt his teeth sink into the soft skin of Aiden's neck. He heard a small squeal near his ear. The warmth flowed through Jerome's body again. He noted it with revulsion, now knowing exactly what it was.

When Jerome finally stepped back, Aiden's body was a shriveled husk on the ground. It looked up at him with confused, pained eyes.

"Goodbye, Aiden."

The boy's eyes closed as his strength gave out. His body seemed to melt into the ground below.

Where moments ago Jerome had felt warmth, he now felt chilled.

"Now, arise, Mammon."

The ground beneath Jerome's feet shifted. Small lumps began to form in the ground. They grew rapidly until the shapes could be discerned as being those of human hands. They rose from all around, off into the distance as far as Jerome could see. Arms grew under the hands, stretching upward into the sky, seeming to reach for something just beyond their grasp.

*   *   *

Jerome stared out of the shell at Morpheus. It was almost like looking in the mirror.

"Can you feel your life fading away, Jerome? It won't be much longer, maybe one day, maybe two. I still want a little bit more power, though, but who is there left to consume?"

"You've taken my friends. Isn't that enough?" Jerome said weakly.

"It has done much to destroy your spirit, but I think I can do better."

"Why are you so cruel?"

"Spiders do not see themselves as cruel when they paralyze their victims and leave them trapped in their web. My words and actions act much as the spider's venom, to weaken my prey, to leave it helpless before I feed. Hurting your friends, being cruel, softened them, just as it has softened you. They both had strong desires that their lives denied them, though. You do not have such a weakness. That combined with your abilities has made you quite difficult to consume, but you have little life left in you. This will be your final night and I've saved the best victim for last."

"Stay away from Chris!" Jerome felt a burst of life flow through him.

"My, my, I guess you still have some willpower left. It won't matter, though. I'm far stronger than you, now. Tonight I will consume your brother. He will become a being much like me. Then, I will destroy you."

\*　\*　\*

"How are you feeling, Jerome?" Roseanne stood by his bedside. "Have you eaten anything in the past day? I haven't seen you touch your food. I'm really getting worried."

Jerome's body sat up in bed. It performed the familiar task of eating and drinking. "I'm feeling much better, now. I should be fine tomorrow."

"I was hoping you'd be feeling up to going to the movies with us tonight. Chris has been really excited to see this movie about kids that are spies."

"I don't think I'll be able to come. Sorry, mom."

Roseanne sighed. "Okay. I'm sorry you have to miss the movie. It's playing in Bangor, so we probably won't be home until eight or nine. If you need anything give me a call, okay?"

Jerome could see the clock out of the corner of his eye. It was only two in the afternoon.

\*　\*　\*

"I hope they enjoy the movie." Morpheus grinned cruelly. "When they get back, I'm sure they'll be putting Chris down to sleep."

Jerome beat his fists against the shell.

"There's really no point in resisting. I've won. Now, if you'll excuse me, I need my rest. Tonight will be busy." Morpheus smiled at Jerome as he dissolved into the air.

*"Ageara! Can you hear me! I need your help!"* Jerome cried out. He continued pounding against the shell, feeling a fatigue in both his fists and his mind. With a silent cry he realized how little energy he had left.

"This is my head, my mind. Morpheus came from me." Jerome kept beating against the shell. "Here I have power. Even if this shell isn't from me, if it's here, I control it." Cracks formed under his fists. He struggled against his fatigue. "If I give up now, not only will I die, Chris will, too. I won't let that happen. I won't stop fighting. I won't let Morpheus win!" Jerome heard a loud pop as pieces of the shell shattered outward. "And if I have to die to stop him, then so be it!" The shell exploded outward around Jerome. The fatigue eased slightly.

A glow lit the darkness around him. A spot of light appeared in the distance, shining like sunrise after a stormy night.

Jerome ran toward the light, feeling his strength return with each step.

"You're actually going to stand up and fight?" A shadow blocked out the light. The features were indistinguishable on the silhouette, yet the voice was unmistakably his father's.

"Move. I don't have time for this," Jerome spat.

His father laughed, "You're so weak. You could never stand up to me, hell, you couldn't even stand up to the bullies in school. Why do you think you're going to be able to fight this time?"

"I may not be physically strong, but I have something to fight for, and that gives me more strength than you would understand. Bullies like you have no real strength because they don't have a cause besides bringing pain."

"Are you saying I'm a bully?"

"Yes, that's all you are, and I don't have time for that." Jerome ran forward, pushing the figure out of the way. It collapsed to the ground as if it were just a doll. The light grew in the distance.

"What do you have out there, Jerome? Your friends are gone. You couldn't even fight for them." Aiden and Chastity's voices spoke in unison. The dissonance was jarring.

Jerome felt his strength faltering. "I'm sorry. Morpheus was too strong. I couldn't do anything."

Two shadows grew in the light. "He's still too strong. When he awakens, he will catch you again. You won't be able to escape. If you couldn't before, why do you think you can, now?"

The light in the distance seemed to dim as the shadows grew.

"I have Chris. I can fight for him. If I don't–" Jerome couldn't finish.

"You can only delay his victory. As long as Morpheus controls you–"

"I won't let Morpheus control me. Not ever again!" He rushed forward as the shadows melted into the growing light. It flowed around Jerome, blinding him for a moment. When his vision returned, he was face-to-face with his reflection. His hair was disheveled, his face pockmarked with acne.

"You know what you may have to do to stop Morpheus, right? The cost for stopping him forever may be high."

Jerome nodded. "I know."

"Are you prepared to pay that cost? Can you do it? Do you have the will-power?"

"I don't know. All I can do is try." Jerome pushed through the figure in front of him. It dissolved into smoke.

*   *   *

Jerome sat up in bed. He clenched his fists, thrilled to have control of his own body again. He turned and saw the clock. It was just after 7 PM. He knew what he had to do, and that he had little time.

He jumped to his feet and dashed out his bedroom door. In moments he stood in his parents' room. He knew that his father's gun safe would be locked. He started searching drawers for the key.

*"What are you doing, Jerome?"*

Jerome felt a weakness throughout his body. His legs trembled.

*"You can't stand against me for long. I'm far stronger than you."*

*"You have no conviction, Morpheus. I'm fighting for something."*

*"I'm fighting to live and survive. That seems a strong purpose to me."*

Jerome struggled to stand. He made his way slowly out of the room.

*"Where are you going now, Jerome? Do you really think you can make it? I'm already regaining my hold on you."*

*"I'm going to kill you, Morpheus. Even if it means killing myself."*

*"You think that'll work? I'll make sure you don't die. If you injure your body, I will heal it. If you survive the night, Chris certainly won't."*

Jerome fell to his knees. Despite his struggles, Morpheus was taking control again. He knew he had moments to finish this. He crawled to the front door. He tried to grasp the knob, but his fingers resisted him. After two failed attempts, he managed to pull the door open.

*"Look at how you struggle to do something so simple as open a door.*

*What more do you think you can do?"*

"Enough." Jerome grabbed the lighter hanging from the grill and continued crawling.

*"I can see what you're thinking. Do you really think you have the strength to make it there?"*

Jerome ignored him, pulling himself across the driveway to the small shed next to their house.

*"Jerome! You're back!"* He heard Ageara's voice in his head, *"I can help you. You only have a short distance left."*

Jerome silently thanked her as he felt some strength returning to his body. He got onto his hands and knees, quickly closing the distance to the shed. Feeling the burst of strength leaving him, he thrust the deadbolt to the side and pulled open the door. The smell of fresh-cut grass and gasoline wafted out into his nostrils.

He sat down by the door, grabbing the gas can with both hands. He tipped it over into his lap, dousing his legs and the floor of the shed. As the container became lighter, he was able to reach his upper body.

*"Don't do it, Jerome!"*

With the last of his energy, he pushed down the button on the lighter, creating a single spark.

\*   \*   \*

*"Are you okay, Jerome?"* Ageara's voice asked.

*"It hurt like hell at first, but I think the worst is over. Am I dead?"*

*"Not yet. You still have a few moments left. Your body is gone, though."*

*"What about Morpheus?"*

*"Without your body, he has no vessel. He has returned to his master."*

*"What happens to me, now?"*

*"Remember what I taught you about etheric projection? Without your body, you should find it much easier. You don't have much time, though."*

*"I know. What am I supposed to do with that time?"*

*"That is up to you. Goodbye, Jerome. Perhaps we will meet again."*

*"Goodbye, Ageara."*

The fire had nearly consumed the shed. The flames licked the side of the house, threatening to set it on fire, as well. Jerome's projection stood on the front lawn. He could feel his consciousness fading quickly.

He allowed himself to drift over the house, finding it strange to view it from above. He landed again in the back, by his mother's rosebushes. As his life force faded, he could feel the energy pulsing through each leaf and petal.

*"If the body is just a vessel–"* Jerome thought, coming closer to the roses.

\* \* \*

Chris stood between his mother and father, holding their hands. Yesterday the charred rubble in front of them had been his home. He knew that his brother had died in the fire. His parents had told him that.

Pieces of wood and metal stuck up from the ashes, the skeleton of a creature slain. Through them, Chris could barely see his mother's rosebush, bright red and green behind dull brown, gray, and black. As the wind caught its leaves and branches, he caught a glimpse of white for a moment. It seemed to wave at him, to beckon him to come closer.

He let go of his parents' hands and walked forward.

"Where are you going, Chris?" Roseanne asked, her voice shaky.

His father followed a few steps behind, "It's okay to let him get closer. I'm sure he just wants to see it up close."

Roseanne nodded and followed them.

As Chris drew near the ruins, he turned and walked along the front, his parents following close behind.

"Where are you taking us?" his father asked.

He didn't speak, just continued walking, turning to go around the side, moving faster. He turned again to go around the back, rushing toward the rosebush.

"What's that?" Roseanne pointed at the white flower blooming high above the other spots of red.

"I don't know. I don't think it was there before." Chris's father slowed.

Chris reached toward the white rose but could barely reach the lowest flowers.

"He can't reach it. Charles, find something to cut it."

Chris's father walked toward the bush, reaching into his pocket and pulling out a Swiss army knife. With a few quick motions, he removed the single white rose from the rest, passing it down to Chris.

"We'll stop at the store on the way to your grandmother's, Chris," Roseanne said, "and you can pick out a vase to put it in. Then you can keep it by your bed. What do you think?"

Chris nodded, taking the rose and clutching it close to him.

*       *       *

*"I'm glad you survived. I honestly wasn't sure if you could,"* Ageara said.

*"I'm not sure if I'd call this 'surviving.' I feel weak and tired. Will I die if I fall asleep?"*

*"Bodies are weak. They fade and die. Energy is forever. Yours will be able to keep that flower alive for a long time. You might not be conscious during much of it, but I had a vision. There will come a time when your brother will need your help again. When that time comes, I will call for you. Until then, may you have pleasant dreams."*

## ABOUT THE AUTHORS

**Jamie Alan Belanger** earned a bachelor's degree from the University

photo by Lee Patterson

of South Florida in Computer Science and worked for a small software company in Tampa for eight years before moving to Maine to pursue his own projects. He currently works for a company he started with his brother Paul, Lost Luggage Studios. His interests include computers, writing, photography, and designing worlds he'd rather live in.

**Shelli-Jo Pelletier** has been determined to write stories for book-eager

children ever since third grade, when a teacher assigned her additional coursework because she "read too much." Born and raised in southern Maine, she received her bachelor's in creative writing from the University of Maine at Farmington. Her previous publications include a chapter in "Telling Their Stories: Women Business Owners in Western Maine," a project by the Western Mountains Alliance to honor women entrepreneurs.

# ABOUT THE AUTHORS

**D.L. Harvey** has a degree in Anthropology-Geography with a side focus in economics that helps with creating her universes. Her pursuit of a Master's of Psychology aids in both the development of her fictional characters and in managing her real life family of five. She has an eclectic range of interests from genetics to psychics, from singing to quantum theory, from linguistics to motorcycles. She hopes her writing shows that the universe is an amazing, beautiful, and scary place, worthy to be explored and shared.

**Steven Inman** finds his many jobs to be an interesting diversion from his writing obsession. He lives in Portland where his B.A. in Classical Literature comes in handy in his daytime maintenance work, where reads Candide to air handling units. He has worked in cemeteries, hotels, churches, shelters, and M60A1 tanks. In his spare time he reads, writes, runs, eats meals, plays with old movie projectors and office equipment, and eventually goes to work.

# ABOUT THE AUTHORS

**Timothy Lynch** is a Reference Librarian at The University of Southern

Maine. He graduated with a BA in English Literature from St. Bonaventure University and an MLS in Library and Information Science from Simmons College. He enjoys reading, writing and walking around Back Cove in Portland. At least once a month he can also be found swimming mythical rivers and hiking the endless trails of dreams.

**Richard Veysey** is the youngest member of the Greater Portland

Scribists and our current leader. He has been telling stories since he could put words together to form a sentence, and writing since he learned how to read. In his free time, he likes to write, program and play video games, make all-natural moisturizers, face washes, etc., and hang out with his friends. He also hates writing about himself in the third person.

**Greater Portland Scribists (GPS)** is a group of speculative fiction writers who live near Portland, Maine. We formed in 2011 with the intention of publishing an anthology, which we have done every year since. We meet throughout the year to discuss writing, publishing, and to submit our stories to intense group workshopping sessions. Creating worlds and crafting stories is a fun way to live, and we do our best to help each other become the best writers we can be. Plus our discussions tend to go off-topic on some pretty epic and entertaining tangents.

To learn more about GPS, visit our blog at
http://scribists.blogspot.com

Be our fan on Facebook at
http://www.facebook.com/GreaterPortlandScribists

### Purgatory Beckons (by Paul J Belanger)

In a world descending into moral depravity, it seems Evil has won. After a botched arrest attempt, Detective Debbie Mason's life begins spiraling out of control, forcing her to question whether fighting crime is worth the effort. But nothing could prepare Debbie for the arrival of Garrett Carmichael, a stone-cold killer sent on a mission of mass homicide by his mysterious employer.

### Pariah (by Jamie Alan Belanger)

Neil Roberts, a programmer for the largest software provider on the planet, stops in a bar and witnesses a murder. His once boring life changes drastically when, through a twist of fate and a realization that his life has no purpose beyond his job, he leaves the scene of the crime and becomes a suspect. Neil's life shifts from protecting people to becoming that which he most despised... a hacker.

### Fireteam Zulu (by Jamie Alan Belanger)

The year is 2254. Humanity has expanded into our solar system. But we've spread too far, too fast, and the military cannot police the solar system. Hopeful colonists are preyed upon by pirates who take what they can with little opposition. Fireteam Zulu is a group of ex-marines who help those people, hunting pirates wherever they find them. Then one day they discover that *they* are being hunted.

**The Sol-Bect War, Part 1** (by Paul J Belanger)
Humanity is near the tail end of an intergalactic war that war
we are losing. After a rough skirmish, a strange object is
picked up by the United Earth carrier Ticonderoga. Within,
the ship's scientists find something even stranger: a man,
cryogenically frozen and shot into space more than 300 years
ago. The fact that he's still technically alive raises questions
of Fate's hand in life and war.

**The Sol-Bect War, Part 2** (by Paul J Belanger)
The war against the Bect rages on. Humanity is now on the
offensive. The Bect send larger forces against us. Our
weapons and tactics may have improved, but our forces are
beginning to dwindle. And the strange newcomer who
showed us a path to victory, Peter McCabe, is Missing-In-
Action and presumed dead. Can the human war machine
complete what he started?

**The Sol-Bect War, Part 3** (by Paul J Belanger)
Six years after the Sol-Bect War's end, peace is still elusive.
While the Bectolothian home world is torn apart by civil war,
their military ignites another conflict with the Terrans. A
Bect spy betrays Peter McCabe, and Terran and Bect forces
converge on Vale-4. With war on every front, spies on every
side, and the lines of friendship so blurry, how can Peter
know who to trust?

ALSO PUBLISHED BY LOST LUGGAGE STUDIOS, LLC

### Scribings, Vol 1

The first volume of short stories compiled by the Greater Portland Scribists, a group of speculative fiction writers in the Portland, Maine area. This compilation contains eleven pieces of fiction written by members Lee Patterson; Cynthia Ravinski, MA; Jamie Alan Belanger; and Richard Veysey.

### Scribings, Vol 2: Lost Civilizations

Join the Greater Portland Scribists on a journey into lands long lost. Scribings, Vol 2: Lost Civilizations contains eight stories about Ancient Egypt, the Vikings, Atlantis, and even a few completely fictional civilizations. Written by members Richard Veysey; Cynthia Ravinski, MA; Jamie Alan Belanger; Christopher L. Weston, and Timothy Lynch.

### Scribings, Vol 3: Metamorphosis

Change is inevitable. Everything that happens in your life alters you, forever, for better or worse. Scribings, Vol 3: Metamorphosis contains six stories from the Greater Portland Scribists that explore how individuals and societies deal with transformations.

## Terran Shift Anthology, Vol 1

The Terran Shift Anthology, Volume 1, the first collection of stories set exclusively in the Terran Shift universe, contains seven science fiction stories from five authors set in all four eras -- from Bio-Tech dystopia to The Sol-Bect War era. This anthology includes The Sol-Bect Setup, the thrilling lost chapter in which Peter McCabe visits the past to lay the groundwork for his future.

www.ingramcontent.com/pod-product-compliance
Lightning Source LLC
Chambersburg PA
CBHW070532180626
46817CB00005B/1804